THE
SILVER BOOK

ALSO BY OLIVIA LAING

The Garden Against Time

Everybody

Funny Weather

Crudo

The Lonely City

The Trip to Echo Spring

To the River

THE
SILVER BOOK

A Novel

OLIVIA LAING

FARRAR, STRAUS AND GIROUX

NEW YORK

Farrar, Straus and Giroux
120 Broadway, New York 10271

EU Representative: Macmillan Publishers Ireland Ltd, 1st Floor,
The Liffey Trust Centre, 117–126 Sheriff Street Upper, Dublin 1, D01 YC43

Copyright © 2025 by Olivia Laing
All rights reserved
Printed in the United States of America
Originally published in 2025 by Hamish Hamilton, Great Britain
Published in the United States by Farrar, Straus and Giroux
First American edition, 2025

Library of Congress Cataloging-in-Publication Data
Names: Laing, Olivia, author.
Title: The silver book : a novel / Olivia Laing.
Description: First American edition. | New York : Farrar, Straus and Giroux, 2025.
Identifiers: LCCN 2025026688 | ISBN 9780374618315 (hardcover)
Subjects: LCGFT: Novels.
Classification: LCC PR6112.A336 S55 2025 | DDC 823/.92 23/eng/20250—dc09
LC record available at https://lccn.loc.gov/2025026688

The publisher of this book does not authorize the use or
reproduction of any part of this book in any manner for the purpose
of training artificial intelligence technologies or systems.
The publisher of this book expressly reserves this book from the Text
and Data Mining exception in accordance with Article 4(3) of the
European Union Digital Single Market Directive 2019/790.

Our books may be purchased in bulk for specialty retail/wholesale,
literacy, corporate/premium, educational, and subscription box use.
Please contact MacmillanSpecialMarkets@macmillan.com.

www.fsgbooks.com
Follow us on social media at @fsgbooks

10 9 8 7 6 5 4 3 2 1

This is a work of fiction. Names, characters, places, organizations, and incidents
either are products of the author's imagination or are used fictitiously.

For Danilo Donati,
and in memory of Gary Indiana

'Making yourself up is an offshoot of our modernity. So I'm everything and nothing. I am what I invent.'

Federico Fellini, in *I'm a Born Liar: A Fellini Lexicon*

ACT 1

ARGENTO

1

He's walking back from the Tate, pictures in his head, enjoying the looseness of the afternoon. There's a delicious sense of autumn in the air, like hitting a cool patch when swimming. He jogs across Horseferry Road, ducking between buses and jumping on to the pavement. There's a hoarding outside the newsagent. He must have caught the photograph out of the corner of his eye, snapping back to see the headline. The rush of nausea is so intense he doubles up. This is not what he intended, not how he thought things would go. He forces himself upright. He has to exert all his self-control to walk casually down Tufton Street, to turn the key in the double door, to enter the lift. No one sees him.

He needs to get out of here, for a start. He needs to erase his traces, to vacate the premises before somebody comes. He looks around the room, the mirror room he has always hated. There is almost nothing of his here. In the bedroom, he bundles his clothes into a bag, finds the neat stack of twenties in the bureau, takes them all. He leaves his books. There's no name in the flyleaves. Better not to weigh himself down.

He will have to leave London. That's the first thing. Or should he leave England altogether? Remove himself from possible questions, speculation.

It's started to rain, fat spots puckering on the glass. He runs through the logistics. Get the ferry train to Paris, all of Europe available from there. His thoughts swim away from him, back to the photograph of Alan's soft, sober face. This time he digs his nails into his thumb until the dizziness has passed. He finds his mac, turns the pockets out on to the bed. Passport, handkerchief, sketchbook, pencil. His own tooth marks fill him with disgust. It is 17 September 1974, he is twenty-two and he has already obliterated the first of his lives.

2

He has buttoned his coat, he has locked the door. For a minute the key confuses him. He walks quickly to the river. It's raining for real now. Good. People keep their heads down in the rain. He stands on the Embankment and allows the key to slip from his hand into the river below. Imagines it falling through the churning currents, fetching up alongside Roman coins and pins, never to be seen again. Not that anything is that secure. Then he turns for the station. City men with rumbling stomachs, bound for Hampshire or Sussex, the concourse a sea of wet tan mackintoshes and bowler hats. In a different mood, he could get into a different kind of trouble here. He's sweating. He goes down the stairs to the urinals, walks into a stall and blots under his arms with a shiny wad of tissue. In the mirror his face is paper white, carrot topped. Buck up Gerald he hears a man say, and an answering laugh. He meets his own gaze and consciously flicks the switch, makes himself alluring, wide-eyed, then turns himself off. He's a good ghost, practised at the art of invisibility, the knack of becoming an object that eyes skim over. Sometimes it's useful, though increasingly he wonders what would happen if he forgot the reverse, the jump into legibility that returns him to the world.

Upstairs, he stops for a moment under the departure board. There are trains to places he has never been.

Belgrade, Athens, Salzburg. Split, Vienna. The *Night Ferry* train to Paris leaves at nine. He buys a ticket and sits where he can hardly hear the newspaper man carolling his wares.

3

It's hard to sleep on the boat, curled awkwardly into a chair. There is a problem about where to hang his feet. He can smell vomit and diesel, and as he shuts his eyes he has the distressing sense that a dimension has opened invisibly beneath him, accompanied by the clanking of chains as they lash cars to the deck. He takes refuge in plans. He doesn't want to stop in France. At Gare du Nord he will find a train to take him across the border to Venice.

He has never been to Venice. It was not a station on either of the art student trips he took to Italy. He knows Florence, Arezzo, Rome, Pompeii. Last Halloween, with Alan, he went to see *Don't Look Now*. They both treated it as a joke, laughed so much in the final Hammer Horror minutes that they were asked not to return. But he retained an impression of stone crumbling into water that seems almost congenial now. He can look at churches and paintings, dip himself into the blue and gold waters of the Quattrocento. Everyone knows Venice is the place to dissolve completely, to emerge changed, or to not emerge at all.

4

His papers are in order. He has crossed the Channel, he has penetrated the Alps, the slipshod rhythm of coaches jerking him back and forth. He has eaten a nasty sandwich, pointing for it, unwilling to trial his French. It is immensely satisfying to him when Italian becomes the dominant language. He mutters overheard words, trying to key himself back into the rhythms, to move his tongue more fluidly. It is apparent that yesterday's terror has begun to tip over into exhilaration. He's got away from London, sprung himself from the trap of the past few months. Nothing was written down, nothing attaches him to what has happened. He didn't intend the outcome, so can hardly be held accountable for it. The fact of Alan hangs in suspension, unassimilable.

The train shudders through a chequerboard of brown and dun fields, punctuated by willows at the ditches. He is travelling across the earth and then abruptly he is skating over water, misty blue water, above which floats the mirage of a city so like itself that for a moment he feels cheated.

The station, despite its location, is squalid. A boy in stained denim is nodding out on the step. Superannuated hippies jostle at his arms. Hey man. He steps through them, brushing away tentacles. The air is like a dirty warm bath. He will have to find a place to stay but first, the need is almost physical, he will find a place to sit and he will draw.

5

It is here that Danilo sees him for the first time, crouched on the step opposite the church of San Vidal, at the corner of Campo Santo Stefano. He looks like Vivaldi, the Venetian priest, with his pale skin, his flaming hair. He looks like a Renaissance angel, though obviously English. To his own displeasure, Danilo's first thought is how much Federico would love that white face. It irritates him that Federico's preferences are so deeply inscribed that he is aware of them before he can discover his own, more subterranean responses. Last night he ate a bad clam. As he vomited, a rare occurrence, he was aware that his body had taken the opportunity to purge itself, and that what he was vomiting up was Federico. Fuck Fellini. Fuck his preposterous scale, fuck his polluting drawings. Danilo has come to Venice to sulk, magnificently. The project is over, obliterated, though since he is here he will perhaps consider making some drawings of his own.

Drawing is in fact what the boy is doing now. He has a sketchbook in his right hand and with his left he is pulling the building on to the paper. There are more beautiful churches, Danilo says. It's better inside. It's Mass, the boy says. His hand keeps moving.

He doesn't need yet another person doing what he can perfectly well do himself. Do better, do best. At this boy's age he had drawn every building in Florence, as well as learned how to reproduce precisely the frescoes that decorated them. He walks away without a goodbye. The boy does not look up.

In the café, Danilo orders a coffee and stands at the counter, brooding. Demands do not anger him, and nor does being asked to produce the impossible. That is his job, after all. What he hates, what he cannot tolerate, is interference. All summer he has suffered in Rome, it seems to him now, conjuring the eighteenth century out of thin air. Every palace, every banquet, every harpsichord, every footman's wig, every bodice, rooftop, clock; even the Adriatic itself must first be envisaged by him. Each object is a formal problem that only he can decode. He makes authentic illusions. He can create a Roman mosaic out of boiled sweets, sure, no problem, or a life-sized whale in under three days, but if he is asked to dress a medieval peasant, he will start by spinning, weaving and dyeing the material for his cloak and cap, even his underwear, according to exact period recipes. His soldier at the Crucifixion steps from a Piero della Francesca, he brings into bodily life the seething scenes of Breughel. He knows when to cleave to the record and when to be splendidly anachronistic. In August, when every self-respecting Roman left the city, he stayed behind and worked out the formulas for the dyes he will use for three thousand costumes, each one of them hand-tailored. Vats of onion skin and marigold, woad and madder. If Federico is the maestro, he is the magician, stirring his cauldron in the back room.

He turns one hand palm up. The fingers are still livid from these experiments. The film is proliferating in a sickening way. The book is too big, and far too boring. It repeats itself, it is making them all feel ill. Casanova boasts his way round Europe, cock and tongue perpetually wagging, and now Federico is so bored he has set the whole Enlightenment on trial. He has perceived the vast impoverishment of a culture of excess and he wants to stick the audience's head into a jewelled bucket of regurgitated wine. Okay, so he can see the fun in that. What has frustrated and infuriated him is the annexing of his own territory. Federico has declared himself art director. His own workload has not reduced. It has tripled.

His thoughts drift back to the boy. On an impulse he buys two sandwiches from the bar, the gummy sandwiches they like in Venice, and goes back outside. Shining red hair. He needs a break.

6

It is Danilo's snoring that wakes Nicholas in the night, heart pounding, one unfamiliar leg flung over his. Sex he wanted, sex has never made him feel bad, but he has traded away his name. He said Nicholas before any alternative presented itself. Now he has tied his face to his identity, when he could have taken the opportunity to throw it away, to reinvent. Nicholas Wade, art student. He has enlarged his Italian too, learned how to say I shot my wad in pure Roman, which made Danilo laugh uproariously as he came. At first he thought the man bending over him was unattractive, moon-faced and looming. He's got to be fifty, heavyset, with sleepy eyes and a Roman nose in that strange, impassive, almost circular face. Broad chest, thick thighs, fat cock, a machismo intensified by the quick, queeny, almost mocking elegance of his hands. Beyond this, something amused, wry, powerfully sweet, like honey in the comb.

They are in Danilo's hotel room. For the past few years he has been a visitor to the rooms of the rich, but never to a space like this. It's like a cavern under the sea. The water sloshes outside and a pattern like seaweed is stippled on the walls. The grandeur does not intimidate him. Instead he feels like a pearl, finely set. He is looking at the velvet curtains, trying to discern if they are green or black as he subsides into sleep.

He is awakened a second time by Danilo kicking him in the leg. Light has filled the room and last night's wine is sour in his stomach. How many bars did they go into? Danilo talking and talking, him nodding, watching the trays of little black octopus and white paste on bread circling the room. Then the wine unlocking his tongue, so that he spoke in a flood of ungrammatical Italian, kid stuff, how he wanted to paint, what he thought of art school, earnest slurred little sentences sliding in the square outside into his own lips pressed to Danilo's neck, his ear, his mouth. He looks up at him now through his lashes. Above the waist Danilo is immaculate. His shirt is made from something heavy and white. It doesn't look like an Englishman's shirt. Underneath he is naked, and Nicholas reaches up a hand and touches his cock, half longing, half fond. He is smiling despite himself, happy despite himself. Where are you going, he says. Are you leaving? We are leaving, Danilo corrects him. Today you are my assistant. Today you are my apprentice.

7

They drink coffee together in the square. It is still very early. Overnight, a mist has descended on the city. He is a young gentleman on a Grand Tour, that is his role, and Danilo is his courteous host. Later, he will play apprentice with pleasure. He looks at the arcades, black and white, reduplicated in every tilting puddle. The lamps have pink glass. They eat pastries stuffed with green cream that tastes of nuts. Italian women clatter by but his attention is focused on the stone. Danilo leaves a pile of coins on the table and tucks one hand through Nicholas's arm. In the space of a hundred steps, they see stone roses and stone lions, stone men in loincloths with broken noses and damaged feet. There are crocodiles and saints, angels and soldiers. Nicholas is beginning to feel a little light-headed. Across the green water boats are slipping discreetly to and fro. You're very pale, Danilo says. Are you okay to go inside?

The doors of the palace are locked. We are expected, Danilo tells him, and knocks with his fist. He speaks for a moment with the attendant and then they are ushered along a series of corridors, up marble flights of stairs, through rooms swagged in red velvet and embellished with so much plaster and gilt that they look like wedding cakes, distantly edible. All the time Danilo is telling him how he will reproduce the Doge's Palace, how he will make what took centuries in a matter of weeks, maybe days, out of papier mâché and paint. He pauses often as he talks, ducking down with a sketchbook on his knee to copy a pattern or log the proportions of a doorway. It is very dark in here and there is a growing smell.

There is no time to do more than glimpse the paintings. Nicholas has a confused impression of winged heads of cherubs, gliding through a sheet of sky, then a gorgeously attired pageboy, his head shorn, in blue silk trousers slashed with yellow. At a window they stop. First job, Danilo says. I need you to draw me the prison. He shows Nicholas the Piombi, named for its position under the lead slabs of the roof. It rises above the rest of the palace, sinister and silver. He can see the lagoon behind it, merging into nothing.

Our film will start in the prison, Danilo says. Well no, we will start at Carnival, but then, and he grins, we will drag our Casanova into a cell in his knickers. Are you finished? He looks at the page. Yes, I have picked myself a good apprentice, and he ruffles Nicholas's red hair.

Last night, he'd railed at length about Fellini, describing the imposition of his drawings, the way he performed each scene in front of actors, showing them where to stand and how to move their faces, how he couldn't leave a single person to do their job alone. If he could make it all himself, he would! But by the third glass of wine, he'd rediscovered his absorption in the film. He set out its problems, proposed solutions, marshalling cutlery and a little bottle of oil to show Nicholas the angles through which his illusions could be perceived. Why don't you film in Venice, he had asked, and Danilo laughed. Because the film is not set in Venice. It is set in Fellini's Venice, and that has to be made from scratch.

They move on to the Quarantia Criminale, where Casanova will be sentenced. There is a painting of a sad Christ with his hands roped, a red-faced jailer screaming behind him. A door opens and they are abruptly exiled into a narrow stone corridor. The smell is stronger here, brine with a faecal undertow. Nicholas, who is taller, has to stoop. They both peer out of the Bridge of Sighs. Then come the cells. Can you draw the doors and windows, Danilo asks him. They are made of wrought iron, shaped into an intersecting pattern of bars and circles, presumably so that food could be pushed through. Even as a little boy, Nicholas was afraid of prison. He sketches a grid of iron bars penetrating iron bars, imagines a blacksmith striking his blows. The stone cells are frighteningly small, with curved barrel ceilings. Some have graffiti. *OliMeTaNGeRe,* he reads, in fine black letters. On the next corridor they have wooden doors that let in no light at all. He counts two locks, two bolts and a bar and feels sick. What did you have to do to be confined in here. Drive someone to their death? There's a tiny aperture to peep through. Maybe you could bribe a guard, press your lips to the hole and whisper the promises that would free you.

It gets worse. There are cells so low you'd have to crawl into them, cells furnished with a wooden bench to sleep on, like Oscar Wilde. What if no one came? What if you were there in the dark, the filthy water rising around your ankles until your feet rotted and your teeth fell out. He sees again the photograph of Alan, and is aware of a sensation like heat rushing through his body. He must have made a sound before he fell because when he comes round he is on his back, his head pillowed on a jacket. Danilo is smiling. I said you were pale, he says. The English are very delicate. I see I will have to take more care of you if I want your drawings.

8

The prescription is Florian. Danilo is an attentive doctor. He has always loved having someone to fuss over, a little sparrow with a broken wing. He marshals the waiters. Chocolate, it is decided, is too rich. Nicholas needs gentle nourishment. Moments later, he is presented with a tray, on which there is a carafe of water, a bowl of ice, a long glass with medicinal red liquid at the bottom and a spoon to stir it. Danilo takes charge of the mixing. A silver teapot follows, along with a plate of biscuits, one of which says *Florian* in chocolate letters. The script seems to have shifted to a Thomas Mann novel. His drink is a raspberry cordial. The fog is lifting.

At the hotel Danilo insists on putting him back to bed, resists joining, is persuaded. Off goes the white shirt. It's like he's been starving and here comes Fortune with a silver tray.

9

In the phone booth, hours later, Danilo has hiccups. What is happening to his body? He is forty-eight, he thought he had himself figured out. He rings Piero first. They have never lived together. Piero's apartment is on the other side of the river from where he lives, above the shop, right opposite Parliament. He doesn't tell him about the boy. It's not necessary. Their life together encompasses many folds. Piero, who made his white shirt, who is perhaps the finest shirt-maker in Rome, and therefore the world, understands more than anyone that every construction must necessarily contain a region that remains unseen. The manufacture of a shirt, like the manufacture of a film, involves illusion and splendid reversals. Also seams.

Their conversation is courtly and conspiratorial. A problematic customer, the doings of their friends. Piero is not surprised that he is making the drawings he left Rome swearing he would never do. He listens sympathetically to a new recitation of the impossibility, the pointlessness, the waste, of making Venice on a studio lot. Daniluccio, he says at the end, imagine you are just going for a walk.

After he hangs up, Danilo sits in the booth, thinking. Federico has tracked him down, has left messages and, just this morning, a vast bouquet of white lilies. He is always sorry afterwards but that doesn't mean Danilo has won. He thinks of the boy going down on him, his mouth clumsy and skilful. It's like finding a red setter puppy on the side of the road. There is a way to improve this situation, to make it work for him. He picks up the phone again. Federico, he says. I have found an apprentice.

10

After that, there are no more afternoons in bed. Nicholas has never worked so hard in his life. This is a holiday, Danilo says, disbelieving. Wait until you get on set. His job is to draw architectural details for the designs that Danilo is constructing in their room. Each morning he takes the pencilled list of addresses, the marked-up map and voyages alone through the maze of Venice.

He never thinks about London. It's as if he has fallen through the looking glass, as if nothing that happened on the other side was real. Only his body remembers, his stomach spasming at erratic intervals, his vision clouding as if his eyes are still stuttering in the moment of seeing the hoarding, grasping what its headline means.

Sometimes he travels with the pack of tourists, frightening the pigeons in St Mark's, and other days he joins the old ladies with their shopping bags on the vaporetto. The workings of the city excite him. The reeking fish market, the light running in rivulets up and down the walls, the ribbons of black seaweed that flutter by the quay. He is welcomed into houses like palaces, houses he would never have seen alone, brought coffee in pink and gold Meissen cups so fragile he is frightened to pick them up. He is the English artist, or else, Daniluccio's friend. Each time, he is charged with a single duty: a bed to draw, or a fireplace, a set of portraits. Despite three years at the Slade, mostly attentive, he has the feeling that he is completely ignorant, that his schoolboy sense of painters and periods is almost irrelevant in a world so saturated with decoration.

When he returns, sometimes with sandwiches, Danilo is inevitably at work, sitting at the desk with the lamp on night and day. Did you take my set square, he shouts, not looking up. No Dani, it's on the windowsill, right by you. He works with chalk on sheets of card he primes himself, and the air is heavy with the smell of the fixative he uses. Nicholas opens all the windows, returns the set square, drops his sketches on the table. I got you tuna. I hate tuna, Danilo says, and kisses him.

If he's lucky, if he's quiet, he will be able to watch Danilo at work. It is fascinating to Nicholas, the way he converts the real city they are travelling through into scenes from a story. Even without people, his rooms are thick with narrative potential. It's the frame, Dani says. The frame and the direction of the light. He makes a garden tucked beside a church, furnishes it with cypresses and a well, gives it a moon, scratches pale blue ripples of light into the trees. You can feel the presence of the water beyond the steps, an invisible mirror. A site for a nocturnal assignation. Here too is the roof of the Piombi, also by moonlight, the domes behind, the pale figure of Casanova escaping in his nightclothes. Look at those gutters, Nicholas says. So well observed!

Some of the rooms are filled with people. Men disporting themselves and gesticulating, their draped outlines instantly locating them in time. The sun streams into the salon in heavy diagonal shafts. The feeling Nicholas has, looking at these drawings, is that Danilo is on terms with the world. Nothing is vague or approximate. If he draws a chair, it is a real, precise chair, even if it is only indicated with a few scribbled lines. It is as if he knows and has sat in every chair in every period in history, understands their joints, grasps the particularity of their carving. The same is true of ships, churches, dresses. How do you know so much, he asks and Danilo actually stops his hand for a minute and smiles up at him. Nico, you have to look.

One afternoon, they take a boat out on to the lagoon to solve the problem of the Adriatic. Surely you could just film the sea, Nicholas says. He's never been on a set, and it is becoming apparent that he has not been an astute observer of the films he has seen. Or, I don't know, don't you have tanks in your cinema city? Yes, Danilo concedes, we do have tanks, big enough to film twelve shipwrecks. But film is strange. It's not like looking with your eyes. You can't just film a bowl of cherries and expect them to look like cherries on the screen.

Okay, says Nicholas. How do you make snow?

Feathers. Rolled oats. Tissue paper. Marble dust. Never salt, it eats the electrics. For *La Strada* they used bags of plaster and a hundred bed sheets. Best of all, Parmesan cheese!

Hail?

Broken mothballs.

Ice?

Water sprayed with paraffin wax. We'll do that for *Casanova*.

Glass?

Sugar.

Sugar?

Salt!

They're both laughing now, in the little boat, on the waves that Danilo will recreate from sheets of black plastic. Draw the island, he orders, draw the boat, and they fall silent, working away, Danilo's coat spread out across their knees.

11

The suggestion about Rome came at dinner. They've been eating each night at the same place. It's a series of small rooms, and each table is set inside a wooden booth, like an old-fashioned train, so that you can close the shutters and be private. Nicholas, who has expanded his Italian in many directions, cannot understand the accent of the waiters. It's not an accent, Danilo explains. It's a different dialect. Italy is not truly one country, you know. It's a set of principalities bundled together, like clowns inside a coat.

He knows this better than most people, he says, because he comes from a small town set right on the border of two regions. This makes him two people, one cold and the other sweet as a nut. Cold for Lombardy, easily offended, hard to reach, and sweet for Emilia-Romagna, the most innocent region, where the air from the mountains comes down into the towns, so that sometimes on the streets of Bologna you can catch the scent of spring flowers. He pulls a humorous, cod-romantic face. Danilo is the best clown Nicholas has ever met. He can undercut and make absurd even the simplest statement.

You should come back with me, he adds. You should come with me and work on the film in Rome. I need the help.

Nicholas has always navigated by chance. He waits for the open door then hops on board. It is easy to smile, easy to say yes. He is grateful, humble, uncertain, quietly ecstatic. He watches Danilo register these emotions and be pleased. At night, in their sea cavern, he lies awake with one hand on his belly, and feels the crack running through him, like a thing he can touch. He's two people, that's who he is. One is a happy boy, stretched out against Danilo's back. The other is despicable; empty of substance, frighteningly dependent on external resources. What happened in London: it is like it happened in another reality. He can't go back, so he will go on pretending he is what he would most like to be. Charming Nicholas, bound for Rome.

12

On their last day, Danilo takes him across the lagoon to Lido. It will be different in Rome, he says. You'll see. A hundred thousand people every day. You won't believe how many people. So no work today. We will just lie here and listen to the sea. He falls asleep almost immediately beneath their striped umbrella, and Nicholas watches the waves. He has seen this beach, of course. He saw *Death in Venice* the year he moved to London, the year he started at the Slade. I went to a party, he tells Dani, dressed as Tadzio, in a sailor suit. When I was your age, Danilo mumbles with his eyes shut, I was working with Visconti. Okay, no, that's not true. What are you, twenty-two? When I was your age I was in Florence, then I was in Rome, then I was at La Scala and that's where I worked with Visconti. You know Callas? Yes, even Nicholas knows Callas. He kicks Danilo's foot. I was the assistant to the assistant to the woman who made Callas's dresses. I was the boy who sewed the buttonholes. You might laugh but it was a very important job. Imagine if she got stuck!

Later that night, Danilo undresses him. You're going to need more clothes, he tells him. He has a brief vision of Nicholas's pearl-white skin and flaming hair in pale pink pyjamas. So they will go to Schostal, maybe. He pulls down Nicholas's jeans, lies him on the bed, plunges his face into his crotch, then rolls him over and opens him like a peach. The first time someone did this for me, he tells Nicholas, who is already stiffening, already breathless, the Germans were in Florence and we lived like the mice between the walls.

All of Danilo's stories are like that. Sly, spectacular, untrumpable. He licks with pleasure, totally focused on his prize.

13

They take a water taxi to the station, marshalling the big card folder of drawings. The train is on time. It's lucky you're here, Danilo says, sitting back and watching him sling their bags into the racks. Nicholas is surprised at his own aptitude for playing the page. It delights him to be dutiful. The cavern under the sea slides between them. The pleasure of this performance, this duet, is that it conceals its own obscene, delectable double.

On board, Danilo turns to practicalities. He sets out his suggested salary. Absurdly, Nicholas had not realized he was going to be paid. No, Nico, it's a job, a real job. There's a lot you'll have to do! The hours, the duties, he explains, will fluctuate, but he will for sure have enough to rent a room. But you will stay with me at first, Danilo says, seeing his expression. As long as you need. He touches Nicholas's leg. It won't be like Venice. But it will be nice.

14

So, Rome! It's his third visit. He watches Danilo appraising the hustlers at Termini from behind his dark glasses. He looks too, and one of them sees him and calls back mockingly, hi Inglese. The beautiful ones are arrogant and the ugly ones are arrogant too, as if they are the richest people in the city, more desirable than the Pope. Another flutters a sarcastic wave. Flared jeans tight around the arse, cigarettes in the back pocket, acne. Not much has changed since he was last here. He cuts a look back in their direction, the ancient look of page to street boy. He's arrogant too, but the difference is that he's been chosen.

They take a cab to Danilo's apartment. It's on the far side of the Tiber, in a neighbourhood Nicholas has never visited before. Why would you, Dani says. It's not for tourists. He lives in an ice-cream pink building on a street lined with hibiscus trees, now shedding their petals. They lug the bags up the stairs to the third floor. There's a long hall. Dani throws open doors. Sitting room, study, bedroom. Nicholas hangs back, suddenly shy. In Venice it was their bed. Now he is indisputably in someone else's territory. He looks in the sitting room. Two green velvet sofas. Shall I? He dips his head. Oh my God, so English, so polite. No Nico, come here, come in with me.

The bedroom is small. There is almost no furniture: a bureau, a double bed with a dark headboard. It's carved with two angels, their cheeks puffed out. Embroidered white linen, all very chaste. It's not a monk's cell, more the room of an austere cardinal. The study next door, by contrast, is overflowing, almost chaotic. It's clear that this is where Danilo does his working, his thinking. The walls are lined with olive-green bookshelves, but they aren't nearly sufficient. Books are open on the desk and stacked in piles all over the floor. Even at a glance, Nicholas can see rarities, things he has looked at longingly in the Institute library. There are unbelievable paintings on the walls. Copies, Danilo says. Yes, yes, by me. It is as if he has walked into one of his own fantasized futures. Artist-historian. Man of taste. Are you hungry? Danilo asks him. Me too. I'm famished. Lucky you! You don't know it yet, but I am truly a good cook.

Since it is Sunday, Nicholas is dispatched to Fagiani to get something sweet for after. He buys himself a coffee first and stands at the counter. He has somewhere to live, he is paying with money that he has earned. It's so exactly the reverse of a week ago that it is as if he has entered his own sequel, passed through a revolving door into a second life, superlatively better than the first. If he doesn't deserve it, at least he can be certain no one could want it more than him. There is so much to choose from. He picks out two cannoli with bright red cherries, and two buns stuffed with white clouds of cream. Danilo laughs at him when he brings them home. *Maritozzi*. Very good. Very appropriate. These are what the Roman boys give to their fiancées when they propose. And in return he gives him a key.

15

There really are ten thousand people here. He sticks close to Dani, but from the moment they pass under the *CINECITTÀ* sign Danilo becomes a communal possession. He belongs, of course he does, to the studio. He seems to know everyone by name, and certainly everyone knows him. People keep coming up and gripping his hand or embracing him, muttering mystifying comments that might be congratulatory or sympathetic. Of course he's popular, of course everyone adores him. It's not like Nicholas discovered him. He can't help feeling small, diminished, a dog with its tail clamped between its legs.

It doesn't help that he still doesn't really understand what happens here. Dani started briefing him on the tram, the latest in an abortive series, and then got frustrated all over again with the impossibility of the task. You'll just have to watch how it works. Cinecittà: it's a whole thing. It's a world like Rome is a world. You'll be fine, Nico. You're quick at picking things up.

Studio lots in his mind mean Hollywood. Marilyn Monroe and two skating clowns, or a bear on a bike. Hokey. There are clowns here, spacemen, nuns, but everyone is serious, professional, unselfconscious. That doesn't mean there's no clowning, but it's the same kind of clowning you'd get on a building site or in a school. Okay, Dani says, nudging him in the ribs. Are you still awake? Do you want to see my bit?

At this stage in the film, he explains, there are no actors. Those nuns belong to someone else's movie. Federico's been casting in London. The process can take him months of increasingly frantic dithering. He has a pathological need to see every face on earth before he can settle on one in particular. He sits at his desk, surrounded by photos and heaven help anyone who thinks they're there to audition. Better if they just come in and tell him about the trouble they had with the train. Or their wife! Anyway, don't worry yourself about that. As for me, I'm two people. The other Danilo is running his costume factory back in Rome. So we won't meet him today. Today it's the Dani who makes sets. Today is a big day. Today we start turning those drawings of ours into things. Assuming he likes them. Let's go see him.

It had not occurred to Nicholas that he would be required to meet Fellini, let alone today. He imagined him inaccessible, like a ringmaster who won't come out before the show. But now they are climbing the stairs in Studio 5, knocking, walking in. The man behind the desk is dressed as smartly as Danilo, in a white shirt and black tie. He could be a funeral director. He has a big leonine head and it is evident that he's been pawing at his hair. Oh-ho, back again are we? Back to my corpse of a movie. He jumps up and grabs Danilo into his arms, crushes him, thrusts him away to inspect and then kisses both his cheeks. The prodigal, he says. And he has found himself a friend, how charming. A little English Botticelli. Nicholas is pushed forward, introduced. He can't quite believe what is happening. He opens his mouth but the river of talk has already rolled on, faster and more expressive than he can follow. Danilo has his head down and his shoulders up. He looks like a bull. He sets the folder of drawings on the table.

Nicholas's favourite moment in cinema ever is when Marcello Mastroianni walks down the beach at the end of *La Dolce Vita* in his white suit and black shirt, looking like the devil, and finds the corpse of a monstrous fish, weirdly washed up on the sand. He has masturbated more than once to the memory of that dissipated face. It goes beyond narrative, beyond realism. It's pure image, out on a limb.

He understands that he is required to efface himself, so he stands very upright and lets his eyes wander discreetly around the room. It's almost empty, a white cube tucked above the massive expanse of Studio 5. This is Fellini's focusing machine, his device for viewing faces. There are headshots scattered all over the desk, and more pinned on a baize board behind his head. What unites them, the faces he's attracted to, is that they are somehow unconscious of themselves, unaware of any outside gaze. There are no actors' faces here. There are street faces, country faces, faces that are radiant with mischief or malice. Innocent faces, sinister faces, faces that are buck-toothed or pitted with acne.

Pinned alongside them are horrible felt-tip caricatures of women with giant breasts and men toppled helplessly by the weight of dicks as big as palm trees. It's almost unbelievable that the great director is this adolescent boy bouncing in his chair, stabbing his finger at something Danilo has missed. He catches Nicholas's eye and actually winks.

They're in there an hour, standing all the time. Dani takes him through every drawing and though there's a lot of back and forth, there doesn't seem to be any absolute refusal. It's after one when they leave. Get your boy some food, Fellini says. He's far too thin. For a moment he's engulfed by the arc light of Fellini's attention. I like your drawings, little boy, he says in English. Then he reaches out and pats Nicholas on the arse. To his horror, Nico blushes. He looks up, meets laughing black eyes, and then the door bangs behind him. He feels a bit like he's been through an X-ray machine. You didn't say he was queer, he hisses. He isn't. Well – long story that one. But mostly he just has to make everyone love him. Yes, even you. He's compelled to seduce. Oh God Nico, I'm tired already. It's good, though, he liked the pictures. Do you want a coffee? We can have it in the studio.

16

The first week is hard. Everyone in the workshop is Italian, everyone has been there for years, sometimes generations, and he is aware of a thick cloud of suspicion, an atmosphere as toxic as the chemicals that fill the room. He keeps his head down and works, does everything exactly as he's told to. He tries to ignore the muttered jokes that he's sure are about him, the conversations that stop abruptly when he walks into the room. So Venice was a respite, not a fresh start. Now he has returned to his own familiar landscape of dread and paranoia. He has to make himself walk in each morning, make himself speak, get up, pour coffee, ask where the fixative is kept. His things keep vanishing. He smiles, he gets more, he tries to keep it in perspective. New boy hazing. It's not a punishment from God.

Dani is barely there, and though this makes it harder he is aware that it's better for him. No one's going to like him if he's just the boss's pet. On his eighth day, the second Wednesday, Ettore, who is clumsy, drops a plaster mould of Christ on the cross, which shatters spectacularly. Man proposes but God disposes, Nicholas says, almost to himself. To his surprise, everyone in the room laughs. After that, it is a little easier. No one rushes to sit by him, but the muttering almost stops.

The best part of the job is when he's dispatched to the city to make drawings. He leaves Dani in bed and walks to the river. The light is unbelievable. He can feel it flooding some portal in his brain, eliminating anxiety, giving him infusions of total joy. The pavement by Ponte Pietro Nenni is covered in branches torn down in last night's storm. It's like a baptism of green, the froggy water, the fresh leaves. He walks up to Flaminio, just for the pleasure of passing through the Porta del Popolo, the black pines of the Borghese rising up behind the square. London is a distant world, drab and dreary. If he thinks of Alan he speaks out loud instantly, even if he is alone, narrating what he is doing or asking a question, however random, forcing himself back to the present moment. Let sleeping dogs lie. Though of course, this particular dog is not asleep.

Today he doesn't even have a job to do. Danilo, grasping something of how it has been for him in the studio, has instructed him to take a day off, stop drawing, let himself loose, explore the city. You're no good to me all tight, he complains. Go out and eat ice cream. But don't go to Giolitti, I want to take you there myself. Meet me at three by the Pantheon. We need to find you some new clothes. Okay and if you're not going to not draw, draw me something I've never seen before. And he laughs at the impossibility of the challenge.

So Nicholas does. He lets himself float. He takes a coffee at Canova, just like Fellini, and watches the junkies by the fountain. The air is perfect, warm in the light, cool in the shadows. He walks down the Via del Corso, strolling with his hands in his pockets. He doesn't have an objective. At the same time, he wants to startle Dani, to show him the intelligence of his own eyes.

17

It's not that Danilo has been regretting his decision, exactly. But the boy is a burden, an undeniable weight in his days. His Italian is good, he's quick, his drawings are superlative, almost as good as Dani's own. But he's out of his depth, an unlicked cub, far from home. Dani could send him away, of course he could, or he could dedicate himself to doing some licking. It's not just the rawness, though. Nico has exposed him in a way he doesn't quite like, a way he failed to account for. It makes him look middle-aged, a cliché, losing his head over someone so young, so pretty. But, but. On the other side of the balance sheet is Nicholas himself, his incredible knack for accommodating himself to what is needed. He does it and at the same time he laughs at himself for the perfection of his performance. It's his doubleness that fascinates Dani, his capacity to see himself from the outside, the conspiratorial, intimate way he has of turning everything into a play that only the two of them can understand.

Either way, the kid needs a treat. He knows he's been neglecting him. He walks up Via Arenula, through the little winding streets that lead to the Pantheon. Nicholas is sitting on the wall, long legs sprawled in front of him. He looks very pleased with himself, is radiating excitement. No, it was good that he brought him here. Look at that face.

Nico jumps up when he sees him, is already laughing as he crosses the square. I know you'll know what it is, he says, holding out his book. But it was so beautiful, I wanted to give it to you. The drawing he presents him with is of an angel standing on a devil. The angel is tall and slender, with long curls. He looks a lot like Nicholas. He's wearing armour, with elaborate pauldrons and knee cops. His wings rise up above his head and in one hand he holds a scale with two tiny human figures tilting in the balance. The other hand holds a spear that he's thrusting lightly through the devil's neck. Blood leaks out.

Danilo does know the painting, and he's moved by the carefulness of the choice, the economy of Nicholas's curving lines. The pinks are wild, he's saying. The colour of calamine lotion. You look better, Danilo says, less pinched. Do you want an ice cream?

Nicholas chooses peach, Danilo chocolate. They both have cream. They walk through the streets together. Something has shifted between them. A camaraderie has returned.

In Schostal, he is greeted warmly. This is my friend, he says. He has found himself in Rome without a wardrobe. Please can we repair this terrible oversight. Nicholas is taken away and measured. Danilo sits on a wooden chair. He is aware that he is almost trembling with excitement, despite his impassive exterior. All those years of dressing people and yet this is something he's never done. They discuss shirts, sweaters. Everything very plain, very simple. A brown and white stripe, a dark blue check. He flicks professionally through swatches of cotton, holding samples up against Nicholas's cheek. Emerald-green dressing gown. Lilac check pyjamas, and then another pair striped red and pink. He knows what he's doing is dangerous, and yet he can't help himself. For once, he wants to indulge. He wants to take his prize home and play with him, and that's exactly what he does.

Nicholas also finds Schostal exciting. There is something in him that craves a costume and a role, to be told exactly what's required of him, to have it spelled out. It relieves him of the emotional burden of self-invention, the need to produce a plausible face each day. Danilo's confidence electrifies him. Now take it off, he says, no longer smiling.

18

Everything is better after that. Nicholas has a new skin, he's anchored in Prati, at least for now. The dazed feeling of the first weeks has passed and he can lift up his head and look around. Cinema City! Now he too is recognized and greeted, now he has begun to distinguish individuals from the swarming crowd. The woman in the cafeteria knows him by name, says hi Nico as she dollops white pasta on to his plate. He flirts lightly, politely with everyone, even the security boys who loll outside on the front lawn, waiting for a big car before they jump to attention, their guns in holsters at their hips. He passes time with the smokers, the gamblers, the sports fans, the make-up ladies as they shop for biscuits and washing powder in the Cinecittà store after lunch. It's cheap, he tells Dani that evening. We should buy ours there.

He's even decoded the uniforms, all on his own. A white coat means you belong in the kingdom of film-as-entity, that you are responsible for its developing and printing. The colour technicians wear white, as do the people who cut the negatives, who bathe and wash the miles of film. The women in pink coats are responsible for the replenishing of equipment. They move rapidly, pushing trolleys, clipping along in their clogs. The workers in the machine shop wear grey, brown means carpentry, and a blue coat signifies make-up.

At lunchtime he sometimes leaves the cafeteria and goes exploring on the backlot. The land has reverted to meadow, acre after acre of weeds and wild flowers. You can find all kinds of things out there, dumped and forgotten among the willowherb and wild carrot. A litter of kittens asleep in a spaceship, chickens scratching at the foot of a Roman aqueduct. He walks to the pool, currently drained, big enough, as Danilo said, for twelve shipwrecks. He is hailed when he returns to the workshop. Nico, you're fast. Take this over to Sculpture. *Mozzo*, they've started calling him. It means cabin boy, gopher. Bottom of the heap, sure, but part of the team.

He loves the sculpture shop. It's like someone sacked Rome and brought it all here. There are columns and gods, innumerable boys playing discus or posing on their plinths. There are no broken noses, no missing fingers. Every limb is intact, unlike in the museums.

Slowly, Danilo's set is accumulating. There are people building all those rooms, all those pieces of furniture they drew in Venice. Nicholas's favourite thing is to creep into Studio 5 and take a disorientating Grand Tour around a half-cast eighteenth century, where nothing will ever quite be finished. The pragmatic economy of film construction. Rooms with missing walls give way to rooms with missing ceilings, so that you step from half a theatre into quarter of a palazzo. None of the buildings have yet been dressed. This pantomime city with its impossible architecture exerts a powerful pull on his imagination. He is always finding excuses to slip inside, to linger.

It suits him, working in such a provisional atmosphere, among people who are for the most part the antithesis of dreamy. In the workshop, the radio is always on, and they bicker about football and deride Bowie when 'Rebel Rebel' is played, to howls of protest from him and Ettore, who can sometimes be induced to dance. Rock and roll, he shouts. Luca, the tallest and the shyest, is always rolling cigarettes, clamping one unlit into the corner of his mouth. Gio tells interminable stories about his girlfriend. He could be in one of the marble workshops in San Lorenzo, churning out headstones for the dead. The workers of Cinecittà have about as much awe for the illusions they are producing as Romans have for the wonders they move through every day. It's a point of pride to remain impassive, unimpressed. At the most, they might admire a cunning side-hinge, a neat workaround, but no one acknowledges the magnitude of what is made here, its uncanny psychic spread. And then Danilo emerges, his coverall so densely spattered in plaster that he looks like a monster. He stands with one hand on his hip, totally unselfconscious, and surveys the room. Stop work, he says, and get some eggs. I'm making carbonara.

He often cooks for them, hanging up a curtain to keep the chemicals away from his improvised kitchen, basically just a sink and a stove, a collection of pans. Pasta, he tells them all, is a formidable resource. For *Satyricon*, I made jewellery out of farfalle and fusilli, dipped in bronze. They all groan, even Nicholas. Okay grandpa, says Ettore, tell us all about it. It's not like we were there. Nicholas wasn't, he says, and since I'm the boss I get to tell as many boring stories as I want.

In fact, all of them are in thrall to his stories. He has travelled through so many different worlds. He can tell them about the divas of La Scala, or the variety stars he used to dress for TV, or shooting *Arabian Nights* in Ethiopia and India with Pasolini. He talks about growing up in Luzzara as a child, or what it was like to be a student in Florence under the Germans. Nicholas watches him unobtrusively as he spins his stories, his mouth downturned, his movements economical and precise. How did he get here? How did someone so accomplished, so charismatic, usher him into their life? The contingency of it is terrifying. It's in the workshop, listening to Dani talk, that he starts to realize how vulnerable he is.

19

Danilo's other life is lived in Trastevere. He would rather it was all conducted in his own workshop in Studio 16, but a warehouse in the city is a way of saving costs, and anyway the wardrobe department at Cinecittà is far too small for the demands of this film. He takes the opportunity to dine with Piero. It's here, in the big flat overlooking the Parliament building, that he can let down his guard in a way he can't with Nicholas. Piero doesn't require anything from him. He understands without the need for explanation. He has large, perhaps infinite, reserves of tact. He is not nervy, not neurotic. He does not have that appalling sensitivity, those big emotions that lodge just under the skin. Nor, on the other hand, does he play as wildly as Nico, who can make Dani laugh more with his antics than almost anyone he has ever met.

After one of these quiet, sustaining nights, he walks back across the river to the Farani atelier. It is 8 October. They were supposed to start shooting at the end of the month but production has already been pushed back to February. It is not his fault. You can't make a world this complex, this exact, in two months, but he feels that some blame has been shifted on to his shoulders, all the same. Fifty-four sets. It is monumentally ambitious. They have to construct the bell tower of San Marco and the Rialto Bridge, the Grand Canal, the Thames, a fairground, multiple salons, inns and ballrooms all across Europe, each with their own particularity of design. Grottoes and gardens, palaces and prisons. Many, many beds. And then, as if that wasn't enough, he has to oversee, to orchestrate, the finishing and fitting of costumes for a cast of hundreds, not forgetting four hundred wigs. He's been grinding his teeth at night, and he can feel his jaw clicking as he walks. He swerves dog shit on the pavement.

Sometimes he thinks this film won't happen. There's always a point in a production when that becomes a possibility, even a likelihood, but this time it feels different, more serious. There's something weird going on with Fellini, something that isn't the usual tussle for freedom, for resources, for control. All his films are made from the inside, emerging out of an encounter with himself that seems as baffling to him as it is to anybody else. But this one feels as if he's gone to war. He hates Casanova, he says it all the time. He's a puppet, a child, a senile masturbator. On one of the hundreds of drawings that he's made, the endless caricatures of Casanova's haughty profile, his swollen forehead, jutting chin and vacuous expression, he's written in large letters: *THE SHIT*. It was Federico who designed the daft little suit Casanova wears to have sex, the guise of an infant. Who fucks in ballet tights and a white corset? Except Nureyev, possibly. Danilo has never understood Fellini's sexuality, never grasped exactly what gets him off. Sometimes he thinks he doesn't have sex at all, that the whole business is a terror to him, and that what he really likes is to scare himself silly.

Proximity, voyeurism, re-enactment. Take those golden English boys in *Satyricon*: Fellini loved to play with them on set, instructing them how to kiss, telling them when to stop. Up, down, up, down, his eyes gleaming, his voice caressing. He loved walking into restaurants with his arms around them too, the little dissipated hippy who played Giton practically falling out of his clothes. Creating a scandal, not following through. Danilo checked. He knows. No dicks were touched in the making of this movie. Not by Federico, anyway. As for the women with their big breasts: the long dinners, the noisy public dissections later. He doesn't buy a word of it. A performance piece, purely.

But lately a different tone has crept in. Before it was titillating, real little boy stuff: elegant, idle Marcello as his screen proxy, trying to seduce and then running away when he succeeded. Cute, funny, immature. Now it's as if the entire thing makes Fellini sick. The film is a repetition compulsion in its own right. It doesn't move forward. It cycles through the same material, dragging itself down into the mud. Nearly fifty himself, Danilo suspects it's more about age than sex, the realization of limitations, the gross parade of self-deceptions abruptly unveiled. Not long before they first started working together, Fellini nearly died. He collapsed on the floor of his apartment and people had to break down the door and carry him off to hospital to be revived. He said he felt when he woke up like he was groping around on the ocean floor, totally lost. The experience has left a blank space inside him, a zone that Danilo feels as if he's being asked to recreate, to populate. It's frightening.

He is having fun with the costumes, though. Federico wants exactitude, perfect historical accuracy but they're on a budget and anyway it has always thrilled him to undercut, to create the greatest luxury with the trashiest, most impoverished resources he can find. It's his own private Arte Povera of the cinema. Bottle tops, food, flowers, trash bags: he is a magpie for materials that might transcend themselves, given the right lighting. He bought the silk in England and dyed it himself, just as instructed, following recipes he had to dowse from eighteenth-century marriage handbooks. And then, a stroke of genius, he abolished the embroidery and lace that would have been used to construct the stomachers and sleeve ruffles – too time-consuming, too expensive – and replaced it with Scintilla sparkle, the cheapest, crappiest, most synthetic fabric you can find. He didn't even bother to trim it. Hundreds of dresses, and under the lights, in the foggy, smoggy atmosphere that Fellini loves, not a single person will ever guess how he did it. As for the increasingly absurd jabots at Casanova's throat, gushing over his chest in pastel fountains of pink and blue: he made them from a trunk of lace curtains he purchased at the market. So no one can say it's his fault that the budget has gone up!

He lets himself into the atelier at Farani, locks the gate behind him, inhales the comforting fug of camphor. No one else is here yet. The most recent work is out on the mannequins. This is his favourite time, when he can apprehend them like people, before the actors enter the scene and take possession. Casanova the tragic dandy, a turnip dressed up like a truffle. Nicholas has told him it's a dead cert, nearly, that Donald Sutherland will be cast. He has befriended Fellini's secretary, and heard from her that Sutherland sent Fellini a bouquet of red roses, a frank declaration of interest. Danilo, who has watched the dance between actors and directors for three decades now, is not convinced. Fellini will find a way to duck his head and slip the bridle at the last minute. It will be Marcello, the double, the plastic twin. He imagines him occupying the blue silk coat, floating on a greasy tide of his own compulsions through the guttering century, and feels a shot of pure pleasure at his work.

20

The other thing that happens in October is the Vespa. It was a gift from production to an American actress, who left it behind when she went home. It makes its way to Danilo, who passes it on to Nicholas. Now the *mozzo* has wheels. He'll miss the tram, especially at night, travelling in a moving lightbox through the outer suburbs of Rome, a voyeur's paradise. But the ridiculous little scooter sets him free. It's bright yellow, it actually looks like a wasp. He parks it outside the studio, unwinds his dark scarf. Nicholas Wade, reporting for duty!

21

The fittings have begun. They take place at Farani. Since most of the cast so far are English, Nicholas is deputized to translate. They come through the cobbled passageway, enter the atelier. There is much exclaiming over the beauty of the costumes. Less so once they are put on. Danilo does not design for comfort. Part of his brilliance as an illusionist is to transmit actors bodily into the universe of the film. His clothes are a portal, not a historical re-enactment. They force people to hold their heads, their necks in a particular way. They curtail movement, they feel foreign.

Not everybody likes it. Two people have refused his costumes: Elizabeth Taylor and Callas herself. Both wanted to be flattered, both insisted on bringing in their own personal designer. The result is that Callas in Pasolini's *Medea* could be onstage at La Scala, and Taylor, who Danilo did not like, looks in *The Taming of the Shrew* as if she's going to the prom. Pure vanity. Pure Hollywood. For Callas he has more sympathy. The vanity of a professional mixed with the vulnerability of a great artist. She had just been dropped by Onassis, her voice was going, she'd never acted on camera before, she was clinging on to dignity with her fingernails. In that state, it's not easy to relinquish control.

These actors, the ones for *Casanova*, are either old pros or total innocents. Some of them, Federico must have scraped off the streets in London. Others are habitués of horror films, or music-hall lags. Danilo, ex-dresser, recognizes the type. You could chuck a tomato at their head and they still wouldn't forget their lines. Not that they have any lines. Fellini is so controlling he rarely lets actors speak on set. He makes them recite numbers, or, on one memorable occasion, an entire menu, anything to keep their lips moving. He dubs the dialogue in later, often using a totally different actor. You can't imagine Elizabeth Taylor agreeing to that.

Today they are fitting costumes for the salon at the Marquise d'Urfé's. It is his favourite sequence. Red, yellow, pink, turquoise, silver, set like confectionery in a room he envisages as a monochrome box, exquisitely simple. Most of the actors only have one scene, while Casanova, whoever plays him, will be on-screen throughout. What this means in practice is a lot of different bodies to get to grips with, including – it is Fellini, after all – a giantess and two dwarves he intends to dress in Georgian scarlet.

The first on his list this morning is the actress who is playing Madame d'Urfé herself, the aristocratic alchemist. Her dress is vast and white. He has modelled it lightly on *Las Menina*s, with a pannier skirt, the kind where if you turn too fast you send a footman flying. She stands steadily, accepting the weight. Her eyes are enormous.

Nicholas watches them from his station at the side of the room. Two assistants flutter round with pins, adjusting the waist. Danilo emerges from behind the rail, carrying a headdress covered in rhinestones. How divine, the actress croaks. He sets it on her head and steps back, judging the effect. Not tall enough, he mutters, and swathes the entire thing in a length of pink netting. It's him that's regal.

22

There's a new boy in the workshop. He watches Nicholas all the time, jutting his chin when he's forced to speak to him. He's lanky and loose jointed, like a puppet. In his head, Nicholas has named him Pinocchio. A street boy who had a walk-on part in a previous film, Ettore tells him as they take their afternoon pause together. Very poor. Danilo took him under his wing, let him help out in the studio. He's good, he has quick hands. He watches Nicholas slyly, making sure his meaning has landed, and then ambles back inside.

It's not the first indication. Last week, he was woken before dawn by a crash. He could barely distinguish the objects in the room: different concentrations of shadow, that's all. There was a second crash as Dani hit a wall. He got out of bed, walked into the hall. It was darker there. He flicked the light switch. Dani was very drunk. He had got tangled in his coat and was flailing about, trying to free an arm. Blood was pouring down his face. Hey, hey, Nicholas said, hands up, like someone quieting a horse. He got him into a chair, fetched water and a cloth, cleaned him up. His nose was broken.

He wouldn't talk about it the next day. He'd gone into some deep reserve inside himself. He glared out furiously, like a bear in a cage. He didn't want to go to the clinic, didn't want to drink a cup of tea. He brooded, violently.

This was Nicholas's introduction to cruising in Rome.

Now he watches the new boy, speculatively. How tightly does he need to hold on? Everything he has belongs to Danilo. On the other hand, maybe he also would like to explore.

He knows Danilo goes out along the Tiber, takes his high-risk walks in the middle of the night, the strange, suspended period when the chaos of the streets has subsided and before the dawn traffic begins. It is the inverse of the *pausa*, a nocturnal ebb tide where things collide. Early on in their relationship, Danilo described to him a liaison with a baker, another inhabitant of the pre-dawn, and how when he left he looked down and all his clothes were white with flour.

What Nicholas does instead is walk in the Borghese. It gets dark so early now, it is so private under the trees. He climbs up the Spanish Steps, passes beneath the Medici villa, goes in and immediately turns off the path. He goes up by the water clock, along the avenues of statues. Stone men, Dante with his nose chipped off. This is what he wants, pure bodily experience. His heart bangs in his throat. The sound of someone following him is terrifying. He speeds up and then, across the bridge, he lingers. What he wants is to be gutted, to be relieved of his personality and his face, to dance on the hook like an exhausted fish. A hand over his mouth, two jerks and he has evacuated himself. Okay. Okay then.

London was so different. The art students – some of them, anyway – were invited to parties. Maybe you played, maybe you were rewarded for your participation. It was how he kept himself going, in the year before Alan. What he means is, he doesn't judge Pinocchio. But he does need Dani.

23

Hooks and eyes, needles and pins. There are people working at every table, heads bowed. It's freezing in here. The girls wear fingerless gloves, but Danilo is impervious to the cold. The middle table is laid out with hemmed sections, like cuts of meat in a butcher shop. The paper templates hang on the wall, alongside racks of coloured thread, each spool painstakingly hand-dyed to match the cloth. It's an assembly line, a factory of human hands. Somebody has put sunglasses on one of the Casanova mannequins. Luigi's dog has stolen some ribbon and is worrying it in his nest. There is no music, just the clack-clack of sewing machines, the sound of the big dog breathing. He is in it like a dancer, off the book, note-perfect. Everything is at a finger's reach. It's like he exhales dresses, a chorus line of red and blue and pink, stretching as far as the eye can see.

24

Of course there's a problem. Of course he can't just make this world and hand it over intact. Of course someone has to fuck it up. He never wanted to make sets. He's a costumier, truly, not an art director. He can't help but be good at it, but it's not the central thing, the core of his interest. Now he is summoned to Cinecittà, dragged away, because someone, who will be fired any minute, doesn't have the capacity to read a plan.

He knows there's nothing wrong with his design. He doesn't need to double-check. The proportions are second nature and so is the scaling. But Federico has been pounding around Studio 5, where the finished sets are kept. He called at dawn in a fury. At exactly five past eight, Vito rang too. I'm sorry, he said. He's going mad in there. He's smashing up San Marco with a hammer.

It would be funny if it wasn't so depressing. He knows there are problems with the money. In August the budget was set at four million, absolute maximum, no further discussion. Three months later, it's already creeping towards five. And Casanova himself has yet to be cast! There are the rumours about Sutherland, the pop-eyed Canadian, or even Robert Redford, though he still believes Marcello will win out. He thinks Fellini is trying to provoke a crisis: not to escape the film, but to back himself into it, to force his own hand, to make things so desperate that he has no alternative but to get down to it. It's not his own preferred way of working, but okay, whatever, he understands that he is only a handmaid to other people's visions.

He leaves the atelier, walks over the footbridge to Isola Tiberina. The river is swathed in fog and all around he can hear the patter of plane trees dropping their leaves. He boards the tram, he lets the tension seep from his body. Flicks his eyes over strangers, seeing them in abstract sections, as if they've been carved. Red wristwatch. Roman nose. He has never wanted to make his own films. He is absolutely content in his own kingdom, or would be if he was allowed to stay there.

As soon as he arrives, he goes to inspect the damage. San Marco is intact. It has suffered perhaps one performative blow. It was just a gesture, not real mania. A story to tell people later, like so many of Federico's actions this year. Apparently he has left the battlefield and retreated to his apartment, and so Danilo trudges on, up the stairs.

He enters, doesn't speak. He knows that people are frightened by his impassive, unsmiling exterior, and it's true, sometimes he uses it for effect. You're right, Fellini says. I'm sorry, it was foolish. This is not what he expected. Fellini is sitting behind his desk, looking like a miserable little boy. The truth is I went in there to think and I started to feel trapped. I felt as if I was being eaten alive. Danilo knows he is about to recount a dream. I stayed in the apartment last night, he says, and I dreamt there was a whale you could walk inside, and inside the whale was a woman, and when you entered her –

Perhaps you eat too late at night, Danilo says flatly. But a whale you can enter, we could use that, no? For the circus in London, the freak-show tent? And he bends over the table and sketches what he means: a huge whale with its mouth open, inside which a giantess abides. He scribbles rough steps, and then a row of cloaked figures, climbing up. A *mouna*, Fellini murmurs, a *mouna* like a mountain. Yes Danilino. I think you have unlocked my dream. And so he is permitted to get the tram back to Trastevere, three hours tossed like rubbish in the bin. It's not until he's in the studio that he realizes he's been played. He has committed himself to making what was undoubtedly Federico's own idea from the very beginning.

25

It's winter when Dani takes a red brocade coverlet from the top of the wardrobe and spreads it out over the bed. It smells of camphor and sweat and woodsmoke, just like him. There's frost on the windowpanes. They burrow in their scarlet cave, the same colour as the inside of an eyelid. Dani is running one fingernail up and down Nicholas's foot, a prelude to something. They ate together, they are both a little drunk. So are you glad you gave me the *maritozzo*, he asks casually. Are you glad you came to Rome? Nicholas keeps his blazing face hidden, answers by flipping on to his stomach, presenting himself for consumption. No one, not even Alan, has ever offered him so much, or made it so evident that he is also a source of nourishment. Night after night in the red and white bed, a feast for two.

26

The shop windows are filling up with panettone, tied with red ribbon. The talk in the studio is all about the Christmas party. It is a tradition that it's fancy dress, and this year the theme is the sea. Everyone has become secretive, determined that their costume will be the best. Nicholas knows exactly what he's going to do. He will play the *mozzo*, the cabin boy, as provocatively as possible, the survivor of a shipwreck, his clothes falling off him. He finds a billowing white shirt and steeps it for a day in a pan of cold tea. Danilo would be proud. He adds a waistcoat and a neckerchief, and then sets about them with scissors. He finds the white jeans he brought from London, which are anyway ravaged, and cuts them too, as short as he can. His hair is so long now he can tie it back in a sailor's pigtail, with a scrap of black velvet. The secret to fancy-dress parties, he discovered long ago, is not to turn yourself into a work of art, but to stay mobile.

The party is on the winter solstice, a Saturday. For the last week, Dani and Vito have been dressing Studio 15, the second biggest, locking the doors even when they're both inside. They have clearly been making use of Fellini's smoke pots, because by the time Nicholas arrives fog is pouring from the doors. He leaves the scooter round the side, suddenly nervous. His breath is coming in clouds too. He stashes his big coat in the workshop and jogs back to the studio, the air so cold it burns his skin.

Inside the vast room, Dani has created an ocean cavern, fathoms deep. It's very dark. Shafts of pearly light illuminate caves and passageways made of convincing-looking rock, through which pass a throng of human fish. Nicholas can see drowning maidens and more than one shark. A director of photography is in his Speedos, a life belt round his waist. The noise is almost unbearable. Even the music is only just audible, drowned beneath laughter and shrieks. He gets himself a drink. The bartenders are Walter and Roberto, as usual, only both are wearing papier-mâché fish heads, painted silver. They look absurd, they look fantastic, sticking up like pilchards in a stargazy pie. He doesn't know what he's drinking. He piles his way through flailing bodies. Now he can make out the music. The bass swings through his body like a succession of punches. What he wants is to see Danilo, or for Danilo to see him.

The passage through rocks leads into a sort of underwater temple, meticulously decorated with oyster shells and mussel shells and starfish. Hardly any wonder Dani didn't come home last night. The whale from *Satyricon* is suspended from the ceiling. There's a working fountain, and half the girls on staff are playing in it, splashing each other and letting their clothes get wet. He keeps stopping to kiss people, to accept caresses. The waistcoat is removed, his ribbon is tied around someone else's neck. The party has been constructed like a labyrinth. The pressure of bodies pushes him through another tunnel into a new opening. This one is a desert island, made of sand, with three palm trees and a castaway's hut. The lapping sea is made out of sheets of cellophane and a blue filter. It's here that he finds Fellini, lolling with his legs wide on a director's chair. He's dressed as Neptune, but he's also put a handkerchief on his head, its corners knotted. He looks very happy, is spectacularly drunk. He's got a mermaid in his lap and another one massaging his shoulders. He beams at Nicholas. Dani's boy, he says in English, and laughs uproariously. As Nico passes on, he can hear him singing it to the girls.

In the next room Ettore gives him a wrap of speed. He has another of those too-sweet drinks, a third, a fourth. They're playing Bowie now. Our song, he shouts, and they enter the swaggering pit of bodies. Sometimes Nico knows how beautiful he is. He lets his hips lead him. He feels like he's coming towards something, the pitch of a slope, a mighty revelation. The song shakes him from the inside. How did he get here? He sings along in English, mimicking Bowie's cockney vowels. You like me and I like it all, it could be written about him. He does a jump in the air and as he leaps he sees the unmistakable silhouette of Danilo from behind. He stops dancing, shoves a few people aside. Dani is wearing some kind of a cloak, and a headdress of a black ship, with three black sails. It is weirdly sinister. The reason he hadn't seen him before is because he is on his knees, at the edge of one of the crevices in the rock. Standing in front of him, his jeans shoved down, is Pinocchio. The cunt hasn't even bothered to dress up.

27

The phone wakes them the next morning. He sits up and immediately knows he is going to be sick. He stayed very late, came home on the tram at dawn with Ettore, threw himself down next to Danilo's snoring body. He is still wearing the white cut-offs. The rest of his clothes: no idea. He's bent over the toilet, puking, when the phone is banged down. He wipes his mouth, stands unsteadily. He's never seen Dani look so angry. His face is white. That fucking snake Rizzoli, he says. The party was the last straw. He's cut the funding. I knew this would happen. That shit, that shitty albatross of a film. Fellini's got what he wanted now. A fucking corpse instead of a movie. Then he goes back into the bedroom and locks the door.

ACT 2

MERCURIO

1

He is lying on his back, looking up at the ceiling. The cosmos wheels above him. Chariot, boat, snake after snake, falling crown. The sky is a deep, dusky blue. Scorpion, centaur, lion, bear. All of these tumbling creatures are emblazoned with gold stars, and he realizes he is looking at a zodiac, a map of the constellations. A brown and white dog trots, tail up, through infinite space. The centaur raises his spear. At the edge of the vault, a boy is falling. He is dressed in tunic and sandals, a red girdle around his waist. There are stars at his ankles and his crotch. One is caught in his armpit, another at his ear, and there are three in his outstretched palm. He has dropped his cudgel, and as he falls he turns a despairing face towards his antagonist, far older, naked, weapon raised.

Lorenzo Costa the Younger, Danilo says from next to him. He painted it and then he died. An artist in the service of tyrants, just like me.

They are in Mantua, in the Ducal Palace. It is the dead period between Christmas and New Year. They have visited Danilo's mother, seen the sleepy town where he grew up. She fed them cake: slices of *anello di Monaco* with its sticky white icing, and the *torta delle rose* that, she told Nicholas, was Danilo's favourite as a child. His mouth still tastes of butter.

The palace is falling down around their ears but it is still the most beautiful place he has ever been. He can't get over the strangeness of this city, set behind walls that are themselves surrounded by artificial lakes, like the magical barriers in a fairy tale. Everywhere he looks, Renaissance treasures have been piled up and left to rot. Better than cinema, Danilo says, still gazing at the painted sky. To catch all the action in a single frame. His favourite is the little dog, or perhaps the carved galley with its red and white sail.

It is four days after the phone call, and they are already on a recce for a new film. What he had understood as a catastrophe, total crisis, turns out to have been nothing more serious than the rearrangement of a diary. Danilo had emerged after a few hours, shaved his face, cooked them both *brodo*. In my job, he explained, there is always a new project nudging at your ankles. Now I have the time to attend to it. And once I've finished, *Casanova* will be back. Fellini always finds the money from someone. He shrugged his shoulders, happy to be confronted with a fresh set of problems. He didn't mention Pinocchio, and it was Nicholas he insisted on taking on the trip north.

Now he looks at his watch, rolls to his side, kisses Nicholas on the ear. Time to go, he says. I don't like to drive in the dark.

2

It is dark by the time they reach the hotel. They have driven through flat green fields, shining with frost, and then climbed the foothills of the Alps before descending into the pink and yellow town on the shore of Lake Garda. The lamps are lit, the streets are empty. They park the borrowed car, carry their bags into the hotel. The reception is deserted. Danilo slaps impatiently at the bell. A man unfolds himself from a chair by the window. He isn't tall, he has bandy legs. His face is made striking by two harsh lines, cut either side of his mouth. He embraces Danilo, gives Nicholas a hand. He is wearing dark glasses, even in this dim room. The handshake is almost limp but Nicholas recoils as if he has been burned.

At the Slade, Pasolini was like a god. A sexy god, an idolized brother-in-arms, a fox who raided the henhouse of the bourgeoisie. Nicholas had gone in big groups to see *Teorema*, *Medea*, *Oedipus Rex*, opening himself up to their revelations with slap-happy doses of poppers or speed. Sometimes he'd find he was physically clinging to his seat, careering through images, his pulse slamming, surely audible. The white mask of the oracle, its horrible taunting laugh. After Oedipus receives the prophecy, there is a moment in which his face is uncomprehending, totally baffled. Then it collapses into horror as he realizes the totality of his isolation, as the crowd shrinks from him.

The memory of it, even now, causes Nicholas to flinch. He's seen that face, he has induced it. On the worst nights, he encounters it again, though like Oedipus the harm he did was not exactly the harm he intended.

The night porter has appeared from a small room beside the reception. It isn't late, but he gives the impression of having just woken up. He looks at them with cool, unfriendly eyes. They are signed in, given keys, but at every stage he seems about to hesitate, draw back, to insist that they leave. Nicholas knows it is only the off-season, but the hotel feels inimical to guests, no longer interested in the demanding theatre of hospitality. In their room, there is dust on the shiny brown coverlets, spread out across two single beds. We can lie here like nuns and hold hands, Danilo says. He is already creating a workspace, dragging the desk to the window, claiming both lamps, setting out his pencils and his pads. Nico steps on to the balcony. He can feel rather than see the dark bulk of water, stretching for miles in front of him. I hate mountains, he says. I'd forgotten. I always feel like they're ganging up on me. He waits for Dani to go downstairs, then runs a hand like a thief through his sponge bag until he finds the Seconal and pockets one. He is not an easy traveller in his body tonight.

I don't suppose the English know what happened here, Pasolini says over dinner. Not someone as young as you are, anyway. They are eating, all three of them, in the only restaurant open. The dish is faintly disgusting, an assortment of boiled meats, some grey and some wrapped in a thin, sweating pink skin. The name of the Battenberg town is familiar, something left behind from school. He probes it, experimentally. *Salò*. Is it the war, he says, trying for comedy, but his tone is wrong and for the rest of the conversation he is locked on the outside, despite their patient explanations. It was to this town, Pasolini says, that fascism in Italy retreated. After Mussolini was deposed in 1943, he was rescued by the Germans and deposited here to run a puppet state under their command. A new republic of unparalleled viciousness and cruelty. So Salò means the town, yes, but also the state that was run from it. Salò is a location on a map, a moment in time, a state of mind, coming and going, perhaps even now approaching in the rear-view mirror. How he speaks is hypnotic: both his soft, whispery voice and the apocalyptic things he says.

And *Salò* is the film, Dani adds. So maybe the film is your rear-view mirror?

Nicholas excuses himself, goes to the bathroom, slaps cold water on his face. He swallows the Seconal dry. When he returns they have the script out on the table and Dani is making rapid-fire sketches on a napkin. Can I read it, he asks, and Pasolini looks at him. Yes, he says, but judging by how you reacted to that *bollito misto* I'm not sure you have a strong enough stomach.

3

He reads the pages in bed. Dani has fallen asleep, though only after complaining vociferously about the light. As a compromise, Nico has taken one of the lamps back and set it on the floor, shrouded with his own shirt. In this self-created gloom, he enters hell.

Salò, he realizes from the first page, is a version of *120 Days of Sodom*. Pasolini has relocated de Sade's dark fairy tale to Italy at the end of the war. The four libertines are fascists engaged in a last orgy of terror as the country slides from their control. Flying Fortresses pass overhead. The locked and sealed castle of Silling has become a requisitioned villa in the Lombardy countryside. The victims are local teenagers, seized in round-ups, while the courtesans whose ghastly storytelling each night inspires the action are like camp-followers, the guards collaborators.

He's read the *120 Days* before. He picked it up as a teenager, hoping for pornography, and was rapidly disabused. Contrary to Pasolini's estimation, he is not troubled by violence itself. He disassociates, absorbs a throbbing spectrum of red to black. What he couldn't bear, what made him feel physically as if he had to escape his own skin, was the horror de Sade inflicted on the fact of being. It made him ill with claustrophobia, just like the prison cells at the Doge's Palace. It's just words, he says, to calm himself, but somewhere in his mind is a too ready converter of language into pain.

He finishes the script, he sets it down beside the bed. He resists the childish temptation to put it in the wardrobe and lock the door. Think like Dani, see it only as a set of problems to be solved, a collection of images that have their own intelligence, their own necessity to be produced. But he doesn't get to sleep until he has stolen and swallowed a second Seconal.

4

Dani wakes happy. He has two masters and they work in very different ways. With Fellini there is no freedom, no privacy. He is simply a tool, an extension of the maestro's arm. With Pasolini it is different. They are a little closer in age, but it's not that. Pasolini works in an atmosphere of calm. He is precise, he picks his collaborators and then he trusts them to do their job. The things Dani has made for him over the past decade: they are more like sculpture than something to wear. Definitively strange, they have the function of dissolving the present, of creating a rent in time.

It is in his work with Pasolini that he has been able to be the most inventive, the most free. Each set of costumes has one unifying theme. For *Arabian Nights*, patterns stained into velvet, for *Porcile* the pleated, not quite white robes, not even made from a real fabric, just the wool wadding a costumier would normally use for padding. He tortured that wadding, trying to figure out a way to set it into pleats. In the end, he designed his own hot press machine, a highly dangerous innovation. *Oedipus* was simply woven rags, hand-dyed, decorated with grass and shells. To get the texture on the soldiers' black helmets he stirred sawdust into paint. He still gets a shiver, thinking about those costumes, their abiding oddness, their capacity to defamiliarize.

The challenge here is different. To give *120 Days* the name of *Salò* means ramming de Sade into a history, a past that is their own. The film will be a masque and an object lesson. Like *Porcile*, a horrified warning. But it is also a return, a haunting, something personal. For six hundred days he lived inside the Republic of Salò. He came of age there. So did Pasolini. Neither of them emerged quite intact.

It is just the three of them at breakfast. They seem to be the only guests. They sit among white draped tables, drinking coffee and, in Danilo's case, eating pastries. Nicholas looks better, he thinks, less feverish. They have been talking about clothes, about the need to convey the wealthy, stultifying world out of which fascism arose: its demure, subdued young; its vicious elders, avid for power. Clothes of dominance, clothes of submission, Dani says, doodling as he eats. School suits. Communion dresses. Grey and white, I think. Or cream?

He has been making his initial breakdown, running through the script and creating a list of costumes for each character. It's so minimal in comparison to *Casanova*, so elegantly restrained, at least in this respect. In other ways, no, restraint is not the word. There are hardly any sets, and anyway he doesn't have the responsibility for them. All he has to do is dress the cast in their respective uniforms, many of which will be rapidly removed. Unlike Nicholas, he has not read the book and nor does he wish to. It is not an exercise that appeals to him. What he wants is to go back to those six hundred days, to lay them bare.

I'm going to make sketches today, he says now. Why don't you take Nicholas with you? He's better than a camera, much more observant. Much more useful.

5

This is how Nicholas finds himself sitting a few inches from the ground in the passenger seat of Pasolini's silver Alfa. He can't help but grin, seeing it on the street, its frog-eyes gleaming. Better than your Cinquecento, Pasolini says. He offers him a strip of gum, slides the car into gear. They chew in unison. Pasolini's clothes are very tight, clinging to a body so lean it is without an ounce, a gram of fat. It must take a lot of work, a lot of restraint to look like that. He knows Pasolini is older than Danilo, who here and there has started to sag, but who is at home in the body that he has. Tight blue jeans, tight denim shirt. There's a brown wool coat tossed in the back. You'd know he was queer, but he certainly isn't proclaiming it in any sort of decorative way. The tone is man to man, unadulterated masculinity, a stance so rigorously produced it feels somehow bogus, especially compared to Dani's easy, unfussy camp.

He thinks these things and at the same time he is aware that the proximity of this tight, hard body is having an effect on him. It's not attraction, exactly, it's more like the shift in pressure that would occur if a volcano was compressed and compressed again until it was the size of a stone. Pasolini is very still, in a way that suggests an excess of tension, not torpor. The images that come to Nicholas's mind are of a snake and, following on from that, a downed power line, whipping across tarmac until it melts the road.

You like drawing, he says in hesitant English. Nicholas is struck again by the softness of his voice. Danilo tells me you want to be an artist?

Well. Yes. I mean, I did. But then I found myself here and it's all been so exciting . . .

He sounds like a debutante. He's better in Italian. I went to art school in London.

And what did you paint? Pasolini uses the formal *you*, something Dani didn't do in even their first conversation. It adds to Nicholas's unease, his sense of constraint.

Fires. Actually. Fires in London. Post-Blitz sort of stuff. Burning warehouses, hospitals.

Pasolini looks quickly at him, his eyes still shielded by sunglasses, then shifts the conversation to English football teams, a subject that Nicholas finds almost as mystifying as his own future as a painter. The relegation of Manchester United is not where he expected this conversation to go.

They have been travelling through another pastel-coloured town. Stuccoed hotels, villas set back behind stone walls. He loves the punctuation marks of cypresses. If Dani was driving he'd say this, but he's too shy. Now the road drops down and runs alongside the shore. The day is overcast, dull silver, and the lake seems to be exhaling mist. There is no seam, no join between water and sky.

He doesn't know where they are going. He's found it better, in his strange new life, not to ask any but the most necessary of questions. Where is the paper. Which mould do you want. Otherwise, he waits for information to come to him, he keeps his eyes and ears ready for it. It pleases him to know without being told, pleases him even more when he finds gaps between versions, multiple not quite allied accounts. Knowledge is power, ignorance is to be concealed. This is a private game. He doesn't share it.

So when they stop by a wrought-iron gate, set in from the road, he merely observes the discreet bronze sign. *Villa Feltrinelli*. Pasolini gets out, speaks into an intercom, and a moment later the gate slides open. Cinema, he is beginning to realize, means always being welcome.

It has started to rain, a few spots on the windscreen. The drive drops them sharply through overgrown trees, before depositing them at the front of a pink and yellow house that is the apogee of every pink and yellow house they have seen today. It is a fairy-tale castle, a neo-Gothic spectacular in Italian beach livery. There are crenellations and a tower like a pepper pot, balanced on the other side by a glossy magnolia. A woman in a black skirt is standing on the steps to greet them. She is obviously a housekeeper, her hair protected by a plastic square knotted under her chin. It's raining harder now. They run from the car, laughing, skid into the marble hall on wet shoes.

Christ, Nicholas says, hopefully inaudibly.

Mrs Feltrinelli wishes that you are very welcome, the housekeeper says. You are to look at what you want, you are to go where you want. I will make coffee in the salon when you are ready. Or you would like it now?

She addresses herself entirely to Pasolini. Nicholas drips quietly, free to gawp. The house is clearly a summer residence, shut up for winter. The chairs are covered in linen, the chandelier bagged. There is a fresco on the ceiling but it's too dark to make out. We'll begin upstairs, Pasolini says, and starts to climb.

Either he has been here before or he got detailed instructions, because he goes straight down the corridor to a bedroom dominated by the presence of the big magnolia. You have to crane your head to see the water beyond. It's very dark and the light switch doesn't work. No bulbs, Pasolini says. Look.

In summer it must be a delightful place to retreat, a cradle slung close enough to the lake to hear the waves, but now the wind is in the tree and the leaves scrape against the glass, an unpleasant sound. This was Mussolini's bedroom, Pasolini says. He was billeted here by the Germans. A puppet in command of a false republic. There was a gun tower on the roof. Nicholas fumbles for his sketchbook. Take measurements too, Pasolini says. I don't think we'll film in here but I want it as a model. I'll see you downstairs.

Left alone, he makes his measurements and draws a quick scale plan. There's a lot of hefty deco furniture in here. He leans for a moment against the wall. It's so damp a scurf of pink plaster comes off on his sleeve. Before he goes downstairs he looks quickly into other rooms, all stripped, all shuttered. One is a boy's bedroom, with model cars set out on a chest of drawers, mid-race. Yellow coming up on the inside, blue in the lead. What a melancholy house. He thinks of where he came from, comfortable until it wasn't, and wonders what it would feel like to grow up here. It isn't old money. It must have been made for some industrialist, some nineteenth-century family rocketing in status as they cracked the code of labour into leisure. He catches his own face, swimming from a mirror, and thinks again of how good he looks among things he can't afford. Better still, to be among them without wanting in.

6

It is Dani who explains the house. They are eating together. Pasolini dropped him at the hotel and drove off, no explanation. He is polite but not warm. Shy, preoccupied, locked in a passionate conversation with himself, an engine with nothing to spare, at least today. The journey back was very quiet. Nicholas and Dani are eating steak now, drinking small fast glasses of red wine, the jug set between them. He is so happy sometimes just to sit opposite Dani, to watch his downturned mouth, the amusement rising in his eyes. Each time the waiter turns to take Nicholas's order Dani silently quacks his lips. He must be drunk, it shouldn't be this funny. He's wiping away tears.

So, yes, you are right, Dani says, when Nicholas has regained control of his face. The house was built for the Feltrinellis. A big industrialist family, made their money in banking, utilities, lumber. Lots of fingers, lots of pies. Just before the war Carlo died, the wife remarried a journalist. Then in '43, well, the Germans establish Salò. They need to put Mussolini somewhere they can keep their eye on him, so they pick Villa Feltrinelli. Then the Americans come, blah blah, you know all that, Mussolini is hung from his girder. After the war, the family takes back the house. The son by now is a communist, Giangiacomo. He inherits a fortune at twenty-one. He runs the bank, but he's literary, he's political, he's involved in all the causes. He published *The Leopard*, you know. Okay, so he gets more radical, more angry, like everyone in Italy in these years. Bombs on the left, bombs on the right. He goes to Cuba, he goes to Bolivia, he comes back home and founds a militant organization, he goes underground. Next thing you know, two years ago, he turns up dead. Cut in half. Tried to dynamite a pylon, apparently. He shrugs, the wholly Italian shrug that functions to cast doubt, to peel back a statement.

Is that part of the film, Nicholas asks. I mean, is that why it's a location?

Oh no. No, I think it's just about Mussolini, but if you know the house, yes, you'd know the story.

Nicholas can't believe how hungry he is. He's wolfed his steak, is now forking up fried potatoes from Danilo's plate. Can we have pudding, he says. Can we have grappa? And he looks up in time to catch Dani's mouth actually smiling.

7

They are acquiring a collection of sinister, peeling buildings. Yesterday, they drove both cars back to Mantua. Today, the three of them are criss-crossing the countryside in search of suitable locations to film the round-ups. Nicholas is squashed in the back, even though, as he observes only to himself, he has by far the longest legs. The Alfa draws attention in the villages. Boys are drawn to it, emerging from houses, fields like so many iron filings. They are drawn to Pasolini too. With them he is no longer tongue-tied. He horses about, he enters into games, he uses diminutives, he is physically far less restrained. Nicholas watches as he puts a boy into a headlock and then ruffles his hair. The boys like him back, compete for his attention. They furnish him with lists of the best isolated church, the best unfrequented square and in return he distributes cigarettes, even allows one curly-headed boy to jump in the front and sound the horn.

The country is flat and damp, green even in December. This is what I emerged out of, Danilo says, looking with disgust at the drainage ditches that line the road. Low horizons. In more ways than one.

They are trying to find one of the boys' suggestions, a farm in Roncoferraro. Ploughed fields, the blue silhouettes of far-off trees. It's strangely like England, the damp in your bones, the feeling that there is nothing on the horizon, nowhere else to go. A ruined villa, its windows boarded up. They drive right through the village and at the end is a building straight from de Chirico, long and low, facing on to a paved square that is open on three sides. It's a threshing floor, Danilo says. It is perfect for cinema, as good as a sound stage. Pasolini jumps out with his camera. They watch him run from one end of the square to the other, crouching to take pictures. Can you draw the pillars on the barn, he shouts to Nico. Just the detail. Then he starts pacing the square out in precise steps.

Danilo navigates the route back. If we drop down to Garolda, he says, we can pick up the main road back into town. Give us a chance to look at some more winter barley. Or maybe you'd prefer peas. He's been sullen all day, sunk in his collar, his face disdainful. A heron lifts out of the ditch and flaps heavily towards a row of poplars, like a coat moving through the air. We just passed a row like that, Pasolini says. The road is absolutely straight. There is no other traffic. He stops and frames the shot with his hands, then turns and makes the reverse. He's right. They are almost identical. Symmetry is essential in this film. Symmetry means no escape, no possibility of escape, he says to Danilo, who grunts.

At the junction they turn right. There's a shrine by the road, its iron doors spotted with rust. They decide not to stop in Barbasso, to go back to Mantua for lunch. And then across the fields they see another ruined house, facing them as they approach. A neoclassical house with a pediment and beneath it a balcony supported by two slender pillars. The stucco is almost black with damp and even from the road you can see the roof has collapsed. I think we'll just stop here, Pasolini says.

The whole farm has been abandoned. They look through the barn, the outbuildings. The garden reeks of rotting figs. Nicholas trips over a bramble, falls on hands and knees in the soaking grass. Fuck, fuck, he says, levering himself back up, mud on his jeans. The lower windows have iron guards. He's shaking one, experimentally, when he realizes the others have disappeared. He follows them round to the front, and sees that the door is hanging open on its hinges.

Inside, it smells of piss and rotting wood. There are mushrooms growing from the walls. It looks as if kids have taken it over for parties. He picks his way through a detritus of smashed bottles, cans of Bostik, wet mattresses. Someone has sprayed a rash of stars in circles up the stairs. The others are at the top, leaning down to assess the light. It takes him a minute to realize they don't share his dismay. For them, the ruined shell is full of possibilities.

Dani's surliness has evaporated. The gear of the day has changed. They bustle from room to room, heads together. Nicholas is dispatched to find the identity of the owner and to locate a phone. There's a run of shops on the other side of the road. The restaurant is closed, as is the grocer. Further along, he finds one of those mixed café-bar-tobacconists that have no direct English equivalent. There is a woman behind the counter, no other customers. He orders a cappuccino and a pack of cigarettes, sips, smiles, allows himself to be persuaded into one of the sandwiches on the counter, waits for it to be heated, praises it and then says, so, what's the story with the ruined house? He's good at this.

By nightfall, many sandwiches later, the owner has been located in Milan and is considering the proposition. What Pasolini wants is to turn this decaying palazzo into the Château de Silling, the house in which Sade's libertines conduct their atrocious experiments. He doesn't exactly say that on the phone. What he does is promise that it won't be identifiable. He has already chosen the house he intends to use as the exterior. What he needs now is somewhere to situate the interior, to create a contained universe of icy symmetry and controlled excess. He doesn't want to film at Cinecittà, not if he can help it. The process that he has in mind will work better with everyone together, isolated from the outside world. It hasn't escaped him that this too is a reworking of the treacherous seclusion of *120 Days*. A month on location, the cast billeted in the surrounding area. Each film has requirements that are non-negotiable. He doesn't invent them, he doesn't add to them gratuitously. He just has to ensure that they are met.

8

He dyes his hair, Nicholas says. He's vain.

They are squashed into Danilo's bed. He's an artist, Nico. I've worked with a lot of great artists and he's the most serious, the most soulful. The most radical. The deepest.

He's like a wolf with those kids. The car! Paying for company with cigarettes! That's where he is now, skipping dinner to troll for boys. Nicholas has a strong visual impression of the one with curly hair and acne on his cheeks. He's sure they're together in the moonlight, maybe getting out of the car, maybe crossing the threshing floor, standing in the silvery shadows of the barn.

What's got into you? Dani pushes him back and sits up, really angry. I cruise, you cruise, everyone cruises. Who are you to judge what kind of sex someone has? He gets out of bed and starts dressing. Don't do that again. Don't speak like that. You don't understand anything about him. You don't understand what he is.

9

It's a relief to be back in Rome. They go straight out, just to be out. I feel like I have mud in my ears, Danilo says. I can't believe we're going to be stuck up there for weeks. He is making another of his interminable lists, this time for the food he will need to cook his famous New Year's Eve feast. I'm starting too late, he complains. Two days is not nearly enough time. This year you will have to be my skivvy, Nicholas.

When am I anything else, Nicholas replies, but he doesn't mean it. Dani's excitement is catching. He wants to celebrate. The city hits him in the face, a rough wave of energy he's ready to ride.

Later, at the Colosseum, two boys emerge out of the shadows. One has a gold tooth, the other wears a gold chain. At your own risk, he thinks, and walks in their direction. It is too much, it is so much too much that it is as if he has burst the bounds of his own skin. Somebody's laughing. Possibly him.

The next morning, he tells Danilo about it from his morning bath. It's his way of saying sorry, of acknowledging he was wrong. Okay greedy boy, Dani says, dipping his hand into the lukewarm water to caress him from clavicle to ass. All very well, but I need you to get dressed now and run my errands. I'm making six courses and all we have in the larder is polenta and eggs.

10

Dani cooks for two days. It's like sewing, it's a way of entering time through the back door. There's no rush. There is simply a profusion of tasks through which his hands move, calmly. He sets up his materials, arranging them precisely on the wooden table. Despite what he said, he did not trust his young assistant with the meat. By the time Nicholas woke up, he'd already been to the market at Via Cola di Rienzo. He bought a boiling fowl and a hare, its fur still shining, and ordered his cuts of pork – head, neck, shoulder, hock – and his string of birds for the next morning. The trotters he took with him.

Now he lays out the first of Nicholas's contributions: the bundles of herbs, the vegetables, the bowls of dried beans. The dead hare makes the table resemble a Dutch still life. He puts on a record of *Figaro* and for the first day he listens to side one on repeat, and on the second day he turns it over.

The first thing he does is skin the hare, undressing it in one deft movement. He pours the blood into a white bowl, along with the heart and liver. Then he joints it and puts the pieces in an earthenware dish. He adds chopped carrots, celery and onion, then bay leaves, cloves, peppercorns and thyme, and covers it with a bottle of wine. He sets this dish in the fridge, alongside the bowl of blood.

He joints the bird and sets it to simmer, then soaks the beans. Next he makes polenta in his biggest pan, stirring constantly. Susanna is arguing with Figaro's mother, whose identity has yet to be revealed. In the afternoon he bones the trotters, working carefully so he doesn't tear the delicate skin.

On New Year's Eve he wakes again before it is light. He drains and dries the hare, frying it with onions and pancetta. He adds the vegetables and wine and leaves the mixture simmering on the hob. Then he chops parsley, garlic, pork fat, sage, and mixes it with onions for the *pestàt*. He washes the white beans twice, shreds the cabbage, and sets them with the *pestàt* in a smaller pan, covering it with boiling water from the kettle. Nicholas wakes to the fragrant smell of meat, makes them coffee, and is immediately sent to the butcher. He comes bounding back with the bag plus four warm buns, eats two of them standing in the door, talking with his mouth full, and is shooed away to his next errand.

Dani slices the polenta. He stews the lentils with yesterday's chicken stock. Then he sits down with a second cup of coffee, and applies himself to the construction of the *zamponi*, the sausage without a skin that was invented by the enterprising people of Modena when they were besieged by the army of Pope Julius II in 1511. The butcher has minced the pork, chopping the meat finely with the fat. Dani dusts it with cinnamon, nutmeg, salt and pepper, working the seasoning with his fingers. Then he pushes it into the trotters and stitches them shut, using the fat silver needle he keeps on the kitchen shelf. It's like stuffing socks. He checks his watch. They have to soften in water for four hours before he can simmer them, gently, gently in their caul of cloth.

Nicholas is dispatched with yet another new list. The last one, Nico, I promise. And get yourself lunch. While he is out Dani sets the table, shaking out his biggest white cloth. He piles it with squashes, pomegranates, grapes, figs. A Caravaggio table. He finds the candlesticks, polishes them while he waits. When Nicholas returns, he sets out red candles, oranges, walnuts, almonds and the silver dishes of dried fruit. Now it is at least related to his mother's New Year table.

It is time to attend to the hare. He lifts out the meat with a spoon, strains the sauce until it is smooth, then adds the blood. The golden slices of polenta are ready to bake, the soup is cooked. He sits down for the last time and threads the larks on to skewers with chunks of bacon. Poor little birds, stripped of their plumage. Then he separates the eggs, turns off the heat, runs himself a bath and orders Nicholas to join him.

11

It is a dinner for Pasolini, to bring luck for the film. The Friulian soup, the little birds. It is a red night, a red cave of friendship, candlelit, liquid at the edges. Nicholas doesn't know everyone. There are people from the atelier, a man who makes shirts. He recognizes Ninetto's curly black hair, laughing black eyes from the films. So this is Pasolini's famous muse. Next to him is a woman with kohled eyes like a magpie and sharp blonde hair. Nicholas is beside Ettore, both of them deputized to carry plates, to fill glasses, to be good pages. Everyone is talking at once, bubbling over like soup on the hob. Danilo is wearing his hat with the ships, a white apron. He is like a ship: like a ship coming into harbour, laden with goods. Nicholas attempts to express this thought. He is very drunk. Do you know you're speaking English, Ettore asks him. Did you mix chocolate with the blood, the woman is saying. My mother was Piedmontese. It is essential to bring the flavours out. The hare is a symbol of homosexuality, someone else says. Always on the run, always laying low. Did you know every year he grows a new asshole. Everyone laughs, and Ettore digs his spoon theatrically back in the pot. Danilo looks at his watch. Five to twelve. Time for our sausage. He comes back with the *zamponi* lying in their bed of lentils. To a succulent 1975, he says. Right on cue, bells begin to ring at the basilica. They rush to the balcony, to see the fireworks. Dani has his arms around the shirt-maker, his hat askew. Nicholas finds himself embracing Ninetto, who smells of aftershave and garlic. It is only as they disentangle themselves and return to the table that they realize Pasolini has gone. It's like being friends with a cat, Dani says, and then, oh fuck, I forgot to make dessert. Who wants to beat sixteen eggs?

12

Casanova is back. It's on! What did I tell you, Danilo says. He feels as if his head might explode. Grimaldi has taken it over, in addition to *Salò* and *Novecento*, Bertolucci's epic about an Emilian estate over the course of the twentieth century. So at least he'll keep Fellini on a short leash. They've all worked together before. He starts calculating on his fingers, how much time he has, how much time he needs. Pasolini, he knows, will not overrun by so much as an hour. He wants to be on the *Salò* set, despite his comments about the mud, the sodden landscape. Something about this film is compelling to him, weirdly necessary. He has to go. If they don't start until March that gives him time to get *Casanova* back up and running, to reopen the workshop, to put the final costumes into production. Obviously there's still no actual Casanova. What a life it is, dressing so precisely bodies that don't yet exist.

He is in the atelier, alone. It's late. He should go home. He's staring at the reels of thread on the wall, each one secured on a nail. He can't use any of these colours for *Salò*. His palette is limited to black, to white, to grey, to brown. Victim and perpetrator. Victim and collaborator. Victim and enforcer. A dynamic with no escape. This isn't a film about innocence. It's an indictment, and he is readying himself to testify.

13

Do you have sisters, Danilo asks. They are at Farani, just the two of them. It's a Saturday afternoon at the end of January. The lights are on. Dani is finishing the designs for the female victims, attaching samples of fabric to each. Good girl clothes, virginal, demure, in shades of milk, ivory, bone, with sashes and buttoned wrists and Peter Pan collars. Nicholas is sitting in the overstuffed chair, his long legs slung over the arm. I don't have any family, he says. I killed them all. You know that.

He slurps his Coke. Actually they killed me. Yes, I had two sisters. I expect they're married now, producing more little rabbits just like them. He can't understand how Dani's mother, passionately devout, rabidly homophobic, can nonetheless accept and adore her *artistic* son, flirt with Nicholas, pat him knowingly on the cheek, while his own parents, rational Oxford atheists, discarded him from their lives simply because he was found in bed with another boy.

It's your schools, Dani says. Everybody knows the English gentleman is raised in a hotbed of vice. It's why you need such draconian laws. He senses that joking is the response that Nicholas wants, senses too that the estrangement causes him far more pain than he is capable of putting into words. Neither perception requires conscious thought. It's their common currency, their shared lot, to carry around the burden of other people's hatred. It's part of the camaraderie between them, unspoken, unbreakable.

1975, Nicholas says now. People can walk on the moon and I can't kiss you in the street in daylight. My parents killed me and ever since then I've been sort of dead. He smiles at Dani, fiddles with the scissors. It is apparent that he's near to tears, something Dani has never seen. It's lucky you took me in because God knows how I was meant to survive. You'd always be okay Nico. You're so smart, so good at things. I'm not though. Okay so he is crying. You don't know all that much about me. I know you asleep, Dani says. I watch your face every day. I couldn't be gladder that I found you.

He gets up and pulls the sobbing boy to his chest. Nicholas is crying so hard now that he can hardly speak. The worst thing, he says into Dani's shirt, is that the other boy, he never spoke to me again.

It was at school, he says when he is calmer, when they are drinking tots of brandy, Dani in the armchair, Nicholas in his lap. In my last year of school. Totally stupid. I thought I was in love.

Or you were in love, maybe, Dani says gently.

Nicholas shrugs, his skin still flushed. The school threw me out before my exams and my parents wouldn't let me come home and they sent me to live in a bedsit in London while I finished at a crammer. And then I got a scholarship to the Slade and that was that, they weren't responsible for me any more.

What did you do in the holidays, Dani asks, but Nicholas's face has closed back up. This and that, he says. I got by. Dani, who spent his own adolescence in a city and under a regime where homosexuality was punished by exile and violence, has a pretty good idea of what getting by entailed. It's not a story you can kiss better, but he kisses him all the same, wrapping both arms around his slender waist. Our life is up against the wall, he says. But you're talented, Nico. Live and work. Work and live. It's the only answer I can give you because it's the only answer there is. And in answer to that Nicholas kisses him back, open-mouthed, his eyes pink, his lashes still gluey with tears.

14

He dreams the costumes up at night, leaving plans for the atelier staff to discover when they arrive at work in the morning. In the day he's back at Cinecittà, organizing the creation of the final sets. The Dresden theatre, the giantess's whale tent. The Piombi, the library at the Castle du Dux in Bohemia where Casanova will end his days, rheumy and confused, still dreaming of past conquests as he dribbles his soup. The costumes have all been moved to the warehouse, so that Farani can be consecrated to *Salò*.

He arrives after dark, when everyone has left. The day's work is hanging on the racks for him to check. When he opens the outside door it creates a draught and as he walks towards them the clothes move, very slightly, on disturbed air. Today, it's the dressing gowns that await him. They look like things the devil would wear. Cream damask. Crushed brown velvet. Black satin, with a vaguely deco pattern shot through it, a grid of circles and squares.

Can clothes be evil? The libertines will begin the film in suits. At the end, they'll wear these dressing gowns. Both are garments of power. The law of the father extends through all spheres, outside and in, from the bedroom to the factory, the government, the bank. There is no alternative to it, not in the world Pasolini is depicting. Within this world no other exists, except as something to be debased.

What he needs to consider now are the layers of participation in between. The people who turn a blind eye, who take the job, who didn't mean to do it but who did. He remembers things from Florence. In the last weeks they keep floating back up, bloated memories he doesn't really want to see. People starving in their rooms, knowing that to go outside meant something worse than the agony of hunger. Denunciations, round-ups, missing people, deportations. The trucks, the trains. The gangs of teenage boys who modelled themselves on the SS, arresting anyone for anything they could. Swaggering, pockmarked, armed. Sliding into doorways, trying to pretend you hadn't seen. The day Marlene disappeared. The people you thought would never talk, who did. And knowing because the next time you saw them, a different coat, a new hat. It's thoughts like this that animate every stitch.

He checks the frogging at a wrist. He is making clothes for rapists who will never be indicted, clothes for murderers who will reappear in the next government, still wearing the same shit-eating grin. Everyone knows it, nobody says anything. How people will hate this film. At the same time, he knows that it is also Pasolini tearing his own heart out after Ninetto, the boy he loved more even than his mother. To lose your love is one thing, to lose him to marriage quite another. He knows that the film is a true story about how things are, the terrifying ugliness of unchecked power, and at the same time it is a vision drained of colour by its maker's own despair. It's a bloodletting, an exsanguination, the re-enactment of a real wound inflicted three years earlier. There is no love, no sweetness, no exchange, only sex as an exhibition of dominance, sex as a source of pain. It's like this black satin he's rubbing between his fingers, the warp-faced and the weft: two things at once, inextricably interlinked. The film is an autobiography of loss; the film is a history of now.

There is no such thing as the past, Pasolini likes to say. It constantly invades the present. Danilo believes this is true. He knows what happened in Salò isn't over. He knows how easily it could return. Fascism never really went away, it just changed form, went underground, periodically exploding back into the daylight. If you believe Pasolini, if you read the articles he's been publishing in *Corriere*, the signs are everywhere. The bombing in Milan in 1969, the attempted coup in 1970, the bombing in Brescia last May, only twenty miles from Salò: all these things signify that fascism is still alive, still straining at the leash. But Danilo knows too, with the same kind of sideways seeing, that his friend is in hell, that he is totally alone, and that the film is coming from this desperate place, this place of desolation. If it's hard to watch, how much harder to live. Make the film, he thinks to himself. Make it like an exorcism. Then let's see where we are.

15

The Vespa has never been so useful. Nicholas's new job is to play Danilo's ghost, to be where he isn't, extending his influence, doubling his capacity. Nobody, particularly him, mistakes this for a promotion. He is still a messenger boy, his master's voice, a worker bee whizzing up and down the Via Tuscolana with plans, corrections, new designs. But it's good to feel so useful. When *Casanova* was abandoned, when Dani took the call and slammed the door, Nico considered for the first time the possibility of having to return to England. He thought about it between rounds of puking, bare knees on the lino, sweat in his hair. He had some money saved up now, but where would he live, what would he do. It was that clammy, bilious day, the bedroom door locked against him, that the fact of Alan's death became perversely real, that he escaped the casket into which Nicholas had thrust him three months earlier.

Now he can't get away. Now he parks outside the studio in a squall and sees Alan yawning like a cat, debonair, uneasy. He's started drumming his fingers, a nervous habit he knows is driving Danilo wild. Each tap is an eviction, go away, go away. Alan smiling, the surprise of his body, unguessed at under the tidy, fussy suit. The yellow smell of him: cigarettes, cologne, a touch of violets if his wife had kissed him goodbye that morning. In the bedroom at Tufton Court, Nicholas once tried to obliterate that smell, scooping their pooled semen in one hand and using it to wash him clean, to divest him of ownership, to make him as much of a stray as Nicholas is. Couldn't be done. Wife's perfume, car keys in his pocket, the job, the club, the parents, the bank accounts, the deeds to two houses as well as the secret, clandestine flat. Alan anchored, Nicholas unstable. He's not exactly political, but shouldn't things be distributed a little more fairly? He wouldn't even let them walk down the road together, so that Nicholas was always loitering, looking at his watch, waiting for the moment when he was allowed to go home.

On the scooter he can outrun these thoughts, slicing in front of lorries, soliciting a whole symphony of horn blows. Rain slapping in his face, who cares, he's free, but when he gets to Cinecittà and drops the designs, he still beckons Ettore into the corridor and gives him a soft ten-thousand-lire note in exchange for the pills he needs to sleep.

16

The *Salò* castings take place in the office in Rome. There are young people everywhere. It's like being in the middle of a herd of deer. None of them are actors. Where did they come from, Nicholas whispers to Dani. Did he sit outside high schools at going-home time? It was an open call, Dani says coldly. They put an ad in the newspaper. It's always like this. In fact, the casting disturbs him too. The way the adult men, him included, sit behind their desk, assessing faces, asses, breasts: it's a bit too much like they're acting out the libertines' own selection process, staging a preview of what's to come. He wasn't anticipating this antechamber to the film, this unflattering mirror. Or maybe, he tells himself, it's just a bunch of kids who want to be in a movie. Best to make it light, to keep the mood buoyant. *Satyricon* was basically an orgy. He's done this before.

He looks at pimpled foreheads, Adam's apples, bedroom eyes, fine blonde hair. Another group is ushered in. Pasolini gets up, chats to the ones he knows. Oh you came! Nothing better to do? Well it's raining Pà, shrug, shove, hungry for his attention. Even the pushy boys, the cocky ones, watch him all the time, half sneering, half longing. He's like a lion tamer: a lion tamer in a brown Missoni cardigan, two knitted bolts like lightning tight across his chest. When he walks away, every eye follows him, boys and girls alike.

Everyone is being asked if they're comfortable with nudity. The ones who say no are told nicely that they won't be required, not this time. The others are asked to remove their day clothes. They dance about, jiggling and throwing poses. It's like a porn shoot, Danilo complains. Can we have a little bit of dignity here? I'm an art director and I require the most superior asshole. Where's my torch? A tall boy moons the table and even Pasolini applauds.

Nicholas's job is to measure up the definites, thankfully after they've put their underwear back on. He does waists and busts, inside legs. The boys make him blush. They're so absurdly young, so tough, so scathing. He still can't really understand Romanesco, but he knows what's being said is basically the English fag wants to suck your cock. *Fottiti*, he mutters. Go fuck yourself. He can hear Danilo laughing from across the room.

17

The next thing that happens is Donald Sutherland is cast as Casanova. As far as Danilo can make out from the rumours swilling around Cinecittà, it was one of the conditions of the rescue deal with Grimaldi, that the film should have a bankable, English-speaking star. No doubt helpful too that the star was already working on another Grimaldi picture. For a moment he mourns the loss of Marcello, the person for whom he truly made all those absurd, foppish clothes. Then he shrugs it off. Unlike Fellini, he finds Sutherland interesting. He's seen *Don't Look Now*, and what attracts him is a kind of forceful vacancy, a striving vagueness that is neither masculine nor feminine, active or passive, but something else altogether.

He hears the rumours, and then he is summoned by Fellini to discuss it. He brings with him the folder containing his drawings and photographs of all Casanova's outfits, from the little white sex suit to the fabulous pink frock coat, embellished with whorls of the ruched upholstery braid you'd use to trim a cushion, stitched painstakingly over netting. Fellini jumps up and enfolds him in his arms. He looks exhausted. There are black circles under his eyes and he keeps scratching at his left ankle, a sign that he's been sitting down far too long.

On his desk is a large black and white photograph of Sutherland's moon-calf face. Fellini has drawn all over it with his felt-tip pens, remaking the actor into one of his own rancorous cartoons. Quite a transformation, Dani says. Will you shave the poor man's head? The hairline has been shunted back a good two inches, the nose and chin extended. That's going to be, what, three hours in make-up each morning? He suspects that Sutherland is going to be made to pay for being cast in what was apparently his dream role. Do you know, Danilino, Fellini says, examining another photograph, I think I'm going to have to request that Mr Sutherland find a dentist to file down his teeth. I don't think the great lover should look so much like a horse.

They work through the folder together. More embellishment, Fellini says, stabbing his fingers at a jabot that already resembles a waterfall of lace. More absurdity! Make him look like an organ-grinder's monkey. I hope he doesn't think he'll be acting because all he needs to do for me is take his clothes on and off. Dani feels a touch of anxiety for Sutherland, who will most definitely assume he's been hired to act. The word is he turned up on the set of *Novecento*, Bertolucci's new film, armed with the complete works of Wilhelm Reich and a brand-new theory about fascist character armour he was eager to explore.

By the middle of February, a miracle, every role in both films has been cast. For his libertines, Pasolini has excelled himself. He's hired one single professional, Paolo Bonacelli, as well as the writer Uberto Quintavalle who has never acted, but has the right decadent, petulant face. For the President, he's cast Aldo Valletti, the ageing Latin teacher who's been hanging around Cinecittà for the last twenty years, picking up work as an extra. It's the first time he'll ever have a speaking role, though of course he'll be dubbed. Still, just moving his lips will be a first. As for the Bishop: Giorgio Cataldi, that old rogue, hopefully not in a prison cell this time when shooting starts. At night, in bed, Nicholas asleep beside him, Danilo surveys their faces, a catalogue of dissipation. Mania, neurosis, greed. He needs to measure their necks. A tailor's job, though also that of a hangman.

18

Casting is followed by fitting. Danilo is instructing Nicholas, playing at training him in the art of the costumier. He is sprawled on the red and white bed. Nico is kneeling between his legs, cock already hard, a bead of pre-come glistening at the tip. Dani runs a teasing finger back and forth, drawing a slow, slippery circle that elicits a groan, low in Nico's throat. And what is the purpose of a fitting, Nicholas, he asks, sliding his slick finger into the boy's asshole. Yes. It's to make sure everything is nice and tight.

Bravado aside, he's nervous. The next morning, Nicholas pads into the study at six to find him on his knees, remaking a hat. Why did you even bring it home, Nico asks. Come back to bed. It's fine, Dani. It's all done.

They walk to the atelier together, climbing down the steps by the white Ponte Umberto to take the riverside path. A man is picking herbs, gathering up nettles and wild chicory. They nod to him as they pass. The river takes up cloud and sky, indifferently. It's neither winter nor spring. The plane trees are still bare, but the sapling that has sprouted on a ruined barge is already breaking into green.

At the studio, Nicholas makes coffee. The room is full of men. Pasolini in his sheepskin jacket, all four libertines. Dani is wearing a suit and tie. He's holding the hat up for inspection. I'll look like my mother, Uberto says, wincing. In the midst of their debauches, the libertines will have a little drag interlude. Their outfits are matronly, absurd, capped by hats that might have been fashionable in the 1920s. You have bags too, Dani says, handing round beaded purses. Paolo, you're getting fat. No more spaghetti or you'll split your beautiful suit. Paolo looks at him consideringly, deciding whether to laugh. No.

The women are easier. The girls come in a giggling group to try on their dresses, their uniforms of pleated skirts and blazers. It's a long time since he made such conventional clothes, clothes so evidently designed to subdue, to tamp down individuality, to confine each gender to its own barracks. The boys in knee socks and shorts, good winter coats all round. Sashes and ties, rhinestones and turbans. The drag only reinforces it, as do the hysterical dresses he's made for the courtesans. A few days later, he watches Hélène Surgère zip herself up and come sweeping back into the room. White satin, huge skirt, sleeves like water wings, embellished with black rosettes, vaguely arachnoid, vaguely floral. Evil flowers, he calls it to himself: a dress that epitomizes the fascist stance. Pure surface, absolute dominance, the absence of a heart. Hélène leans into the mirror, scoops back her hair, tries out a laugh. I hate it, she says. It makes my blood run cold, and Pasolini smiles.

19

Every outfit has to be adjusted and then every character's wardrobe has to be labelled and packed. The shoot starts on 3 March. It will last six weeks. Do I even have a job title, Nicholas asks. What do you want, your own chair that says *Mozzo*? A caravan? Your job is assistant to the costume designer and right now – Oh Dani no, Nicholas says, laughing as he pushes him off. Not again! I've got thirty-six coats to wrap.

20

Dani is folding shirts into his own small case. Bring everything you could possibly want, he tells Nico. I might have to come back to Rome, but if I do I'll need you up there.

Nicholas is excited. He's been working in cinema, so-called, for nearly six months and in all that time he has never seen anyone pick up a camera, let alone *direct* an *actor* in a *scene*. The other productions at Cinecittà he discounts as merely peripheral. He wants to see a film he's worked on, thought about, transition from an accumulation of objects into a moving world. Cut, he mutters to himself. Action.

There has been a lot of back and forth about the car. Should they go up in one of the production vehicles or drive themselves? The latter, it's decided, because of the probability of Dani being needed on *Casanova* between now and mid-April. But not the Fiat, Nico pleads. I can't fold my knees up for seven hours. Why are Italians so obsessed with tiny cars? Because we like to look impressive climbing out of them, Dani says.

What production ends up giving them is a Jeep, another bizarre vehicle left over from a shoot. It's the milky yellow of crème anglaise, with a strip of wood panelling down the side. A dumb American car, Dani says, surveying it, but it adds to Nicholas's sense that something new is on its way. It feels like we're going on holiday. Look, he says, jumping into the back to demonstrate, we can sleep in here if we need to. Or bring home a deer, Dani says gloomily.

On the road out of Rome, Sunday morning, sheeting rain, the big car feels like their own private sitting room, fuggy and warm. Nicholas curls himself up, pressing his feet against Dani's thigh. Couldn't do this in a Cinquecento. It's like we're in a road movie, and he laughs at the dumbness of what he's said.

Hill towns, olive groves, castles tick by. They stop just north of Florence for lunch, at a restaurant in Pratolino. It doesn't look like much of anything from outside, but inside it's like a tavern from a hundred years ago. They're greeted and directed to a dining room at the back. It's glassed on two sides, so that it seems to hang suspended above a receding prospect of mountains, growing progressively more blue. It's been here since the eighteenth century, Dani says. Casanova could have eaten here, let alone all those Nazis. I hope that famous appetite of yours is working, because these are the best steaks in the whole of Tuscany. Certainly the biggest.

They must have eaten half a cow. Nicholas can barely stand upright, but there's one more thing Dani wants to show him, on what he describes as their last day of freedom. They walk down a path, stepping into the view they've just been gazing over. It could be an English park, the orderly, decorous groups of trees. They skirt a villa, and emerge through a thicket on to a lake. Nicholas, who has been kicking a conker, looks up and finds himself staring at a giant. The Colosso dell'Appennino, Dani says. A masterpiece of the Renaissance. Made by Giambologna. Look at him. Even older than me! The giant is crouched above the murky surface of the lake. He's made of stone but his hair and beard, his eyebrows, even patches of his skin are fashioned out of a rougher kind of rock that looks alive, accretive, calcareous. It's as if he has burst through the hill and not yet dusted himself off. It can't be cement, Nicholas says. What is it?

It's lava, Dani says. He's supposed to be the spirit of the mountains. Animate-inanimate. A being on the edge. There are caves underneath him but I think they're flooded. It takes Nicholas a moment to notice that the giant's hand is petting a dragon. Its tongue is protruding. Perhaps he's choking it? He has a strong sense that there is more to this scene than he is capable of understanding, that they have wandered into a landscape of mysteries, only to find the key has been misplaced.

21

The boy stumbles down the bank and runs flat out along the river bed. Now, Pasolini calls, and he drops to the ground. They have been here two hours, sitting on the bridge while one of the victims fails and fails to escape. It is hard to make the fall look real. For the second time, Pasolini runs down the bank himself, races beside the glinting water. He stumbles, recovers himself, then goes down hard, hitting the gravel on his side. Like you are taking a tackle, he says to Marco. You have to twist a little, I think, and the boy nods. Okay, he calls to the men on the bridge. One more. We're coming back up.

It's a full Nazi re-enactment today. The helmeted soldiers with their machine guns are sitting with their backs against the parapet, waiting for their chance to shoot. It's not raining, but the air is full of moisture, settling on coats and hair, glowing in the thin sunlight. The men that tend to the camera huddle. Dani brushes the dirt from Marco's jacket, reties his goose-grey scarf. That's exactly what I'd do, Nicholas thinks. Die, rather than be caught.

They've started the film out of sequence, with a scene a few pages from the beginning of the script Nicholas read. On the other side of the bridge is the village of Gardeletta. Today it has a new sign: *Marzabotto*. Some of the crew are uneasy about this. No one complains, but Nicholas watches one man spit discreetly as he passes the sign. Marzabotto was the site of the biggest civilian massacre in the whole country. Maybe five hundred, maybe a thousand people were shot there by SS soldiers, then a few days later they shot the priest for trying to bury the dead. Like the town of Salò itself, its presence in the film is a way of lashing de Sade's fiction to Italy's own past.

Marco runs again, slithers on the gravel, dives. Grey stone, green mountains, grey sky, green trees. He looks very small. For a moment nobody speaks. Pasolini claps his hands. Okay, we've got it. Marco, you can come back up. And already he's running down the bank to get the reverse shot, crouching where the body was to film the soldiers climbing back into their cars, the convoy passing out of view, the empty bridge.

22

There's no time to brood. Everything has to be packed back up and driven to the villa outside Mantua, the stand-in for de Sade's castle of Silling where they'll be based for the next three weeks. People are billeted in houses all around, but Nico and Dani have been assigned to the villa itself. Well, we did find it, Dani says. Who else is in there, Nicholas asks and Dani consults his list. Core crew, he says. AD, script supervisor, Sergio, he's special effects, couple of camera people, us and Pasolini. And Dante, of course. You met him, he's doing the sets. Okay for you, princess? I think they've cleaned it out a bit.

It's dusk when they arrive, dusk like the bloom on a plum. A small sharp moon, inconsequential among a spray of stars so dense Nicholas almost loses his footing. The mist is low on the ground, the sky absolutely clear. Fuck me, it's cold, Dani says. I need your, what do you call it, *bobble hat*.

Inside, the villa is transformed. Dani is hugging Dante, pulling Nicholas over, doing his usual mocking introductions. Why did you ruin my house, he says. I was looking forward to puking down the stairs. Oh, you can definitely do that, says Dante, beaming at him. You want a tour? I always had a feeling hell would be so beautiful it would make you puke with fear.

This thought has never occurred to Nicholas, who has his own well-thumbed images of hell. But he can see, looking around the salon, that Dante has a point. It's the coldest, most unrelenting room he's ever been in, its scale inhuman. Mirror reflects mirror, door opposes door. Each is twice the height of Nicholas. I always hated art deco, Dani says. Those light fittings are obscene. And the carpet! Pure Bauhaus. Is it Bauhaus? He bends down and looks at the weave. No. A very nice fake, though. Thank you, says Dante, inclining his head. And now: your room?

They're in the old servants' quarters, in the half of the house that still has a roof. It's freezing. Lucky we brought all those coats, Dani says. We can build a nest. Energy is humming off him. Always vital, he is vibrating with purpose and happiness. I have to look at the pigsty they've put my costumes in, he says now, setting his case on the bed. I'm not joking. I think the costume department is an actual pigsty. You don't need to come, Nicholas. I like to do this bit by myself. I'll see you at dinner, all right?

Left alone in the room, Nicholas opens his own case, realizes there's no furniture except the bed, recloses the lid. He sits down, stands up, walks to the window, drumming his fingers all the time. Go away, go away, go away, but Alan doesn't want to be outrun. Eating, sleeping, working, every action contaminated by this presence from the past. Is this what haunting feels like, someone at the corner of your vision every moment of the day?

23

At breakfast, the conversation is about shit. The middle part of the film is titled the cycle of excrement, for obvious Sadean reasons. Since many people will be participating in the eating of shit, the special effects team need to find a way of making a palatable substitute. Sergio is describing to Dani his experiments so far. Chocolate, of course, mixed with broken biscuits. The problem is that even the finest Swiss melts under the lights. And the consistency, it isn't quite right. No, Dani says thoughtfully. You need something glossy. Olive oil? And okay, what about marmalade, to bind it? This is the most disgusting conversation I've ever heard, Nico says, reaching for a *crostata*. They both look at him, surprised. Most of the time my job is making heads that explode, Sergio says. Or eyes that burst. I mean, wait till you see the end of the film. Personally I think a scalping is much nastier than a few turds. Nicholas picks up his pastry and backs away from the table. I'm eating, he says. It's totally gross. We'll put you on turd duty, Sergio says, and then, turning to Dani, but the real problem is how to shape them. You can't just pat them. They have to be extruded. Welcome to cinema, Dani shouts at Nicholas's retreating back. We're not perverts, we're labourers in the dream factory!

24

Outside, a mist has settled. The famous Po Valley mist, which, as Dani keeps telling people, descends without warning and doesn't lift until May. He has muffled himself in a cashmere scarf, he is wearing a hat. Still he can feel the cold seeping from the sodden air, the sodden ground into his bones.

He claps his hands together as he walks. The pigsty is his kingdom. It has been swept and whitewashed, lined with shelves. He has commandeered a space heater, he has two irons, a table for shoes and another for hats. Now he walks along the racks, checking that nothing has been forgotten. Today they shoot the first of the round-ups. Six SS soldiers in uniforms, four agents of the OVRA, the fascist secret police, in long pale trenches and trilbies like his. And the boys on their bikes, the frightened country boys in their newsboy caps.

A shout alerts him. The bus is leaving. He doesn't rush. He locks the shed, walks out into the yard, with the curious feeling that each step is taking him not across but down, into the past.

The boys are wild on the bus. They've probably never been out of Rome in their lives. These three are the advance guard. The others are arriving later today or tomorrow.

It's an hour's drive to the location, along hypnotic miles of straight road through flat fields. They park across from the church, under a willow. The trucks are already here, and so too is the Alfa. You know, tomorrow I think I'll dress the kids before we leave, he says to the AD as they climb down the steps. It's too cold and I won't be able to do so many in the lorry. Come on *ragazzi*, he says, grabbing two of them by the collar. Time for your round-up.

Nicholas is doing the soldiers at the other end of the lorry. Big hulking extras in rented uniforms and clomping boots. Belt them tightly, Dani tells him. And make sure the gas masks hang from the left shoulder, not the right. The canisters should be slapping them on the arse, okay? Not at the side. He does the OVRA men himself. Three goons, one boss, younger than the rest, more dandyish, in a Prince of Wales suit and discreetly striped tie. He pops the coat collar. And don't tie your mac up, he says to the man. It looks nastier, more arrogant that way.

Once everyone is dressed, he steps outside, leaning against the lorry. They're just across the river from Sabbioneta. The mist hasn't quite lifted and the water is running high between saturated fields. If he crouches, he can see the town reflected in it, the pink and green houses wavering beneath dry brown reeds. They're setting up the ambush on the bridge. One truck, one car, a few soldiers, that's all it took, once a state of terror had been established. He was the same age as those boys, less than twenty miles from here. The memory of coming around a corner and seeing something – a soldier, a corpse, someone hanging from a tree: it's still inside him, a piece of gristle he can't quite swallow. He stands by the truck, immobile, watching the familiar little drama play out. Again and again the boys ride past the church, see the ambush, hesitate, wheel round. Again and again, the black car cuts them off. Again and again, the agent smiles, holding up his pistol. *Dove vai?* And the stupid boy smiles back.

25

The next day the same. They film at the grain yard in Roncoferraro, the threshing floor they found in December. Soldiers march past a corpse, kids hang about. The soldiers drag a teenaged boy out of his house, followed by his frantic mother, trying to tie a scarf around his neck. Go away, he snarls at her. Two smaller boys are playing on a swing, visible through the open door of the barn. Bare knees. They watch as another young man is led away. He wears a tweed jacket. *Ciao Ezio*, the little boy says. Ezio looks back at him, over his shoulder. He has a soft, gentle face. *Ciao Luigi*. The sound of marching feet on gravel.

It is Pasolini's birthday. Steak for dinner.

26

The house is crawling with people. It's like a miniature Cinecittà in the Lombardy fields. They're done with exteriors for the time being. For the next fortnight, everything will happen here, in Dante's unsettling suite of rooms. There's a cast of thirty-six in many of the scenes, arranged like figures in a fresco. Each body has to be dressed and choreographed, even if the person never has a line of dialogue. Dani has furnished the kids with fluffy dressing gowns to wear between takes, dipped in the vats of jewel-coloured dye he was using on *Casanova*. They look like a flock of parakeets, pink, scarlet, emerald and blue.

The courtesans practically live in the stable that has been given over to make-up, gossiping as their hair is curled, their eyelids painted. Nicholas zips and smooths; he even learns how to stitch a seam. The crew have almost all worked with Pasolini before. Things proceed swiftly, task by task, then stall for hours. When this happens, Pasolini doesn't lose his temper, but nor can he slow down. He finds the next possible action. He's calm but he can't tolerate stopping. He runs everywhere, the Arriflex held lightly at his shoulder.

The strangest thing for Nicholas is that no matter what's happening on set – a rape, a murder, the abasement of naked bodies – it is all treated with absolute neutrality, as if it's just so much matter to animate and light. Well of course, Dani says, when he points it out. Think about it. We've all been doing this for decades. One week a battle, the next week a wedding. All we need to think about is how to make it look good on film. That's our job. We're the builders, not the viewers. It isn't exactly a lie. What the film has brought up has nothing to do with the specific cruelties they've been depicting. A successful illusion is always a source of delight for him. It's more that the film has opened a door on to the past, and something is moving, down there in the dark.

When he isn't needed, Nicholas lurks uneasily at the edge of the salon, eavesdropping on conversations about lights, a long discussion over whether the lens should be changed. The camera requires constant tending. Move to the left Giuliana, Pasolini says in his soft voice. I can't quite see you. It's like watching surgeons mid-procedure, the quiet chat, the occasional laughter. No one complains about blood on the floor in an operating theatre, either.

Mostly, he watches the boys. He can't quite distinguish them all. They move in a pack, they're like electric eels or maybe bullocks, jostling, fighting, knocking things over, constantly restless, their eyes always moving. Pasolini calms them. He treats them like adults, giving them direction in a way that draws flatteringly on an assumption of their maturity, their capacity for subtle understanding. It's amazing to watch them focus, hypnotized by his gentle attention. The minute the scene is done they're off again, barging and catcalling.

Nicholas is the same age as the oldest ones, but he's not part of them. His alliance with Dani sets him on the side of the grown-ups, the adults. His job is to marshal them into their clothes, to stand by with his iron, pressing shirts and summer dresses while at the corner of his eye a girl spits fake blood into a bowl. Are my teeth red?

At lunchtime, Rocco scoops a turd from a leftover plate and smears it on to another boy's sandwich. He eats it with relish. It's tasty, dumbass, he says. Try it with ham. They're not filming. This is their personal script. The nudity doesn't seem to affect them, and nor do the things they're called upon to do. It's all a source of entertainment, raw material to take up and reuse in their own, more crucial games.

Most of them are straight; most of them are fixated on the girls. It doesn't stop them flirting with Pasolini. The worst is Rocco. He's the kind of boy Nicholas has always hated, vicious to those beneath him, craven to those above. It's obvious that Pasolini dotes on him. Doesn't he get that Rocco is straight, Nicholas says to Dani in the partial privacy of the pig shed. I watched him feeling up Tatiana while we were on set. I think, Dani says delicately, that our friend Rocco might be a bit more flexible than that.

27

Four minutes later, Dani stops outside the pig shed, watching Nicholas now that he believes himself to be alone. He walks to the door, taps it, walks back three steps, repeats the procedure. He doesn't seem to sleep at all. At night, his skin gives off a high metallic smell. What the fuck, thinks Dani to himself, is going on? It's not so unusual for people to lose it on shoots, especially when they're confined to one location, but Nicholas has always seemed so capable, so self-aware, even when sad. He's lost weight again, he startles when you speak to him. There's no prospect of leaving the shoot early, not both of them. Dani will just have to add protector to his list of duties.

28

The café over the road where Nicholas made his enquiries has been requisitioned by the crew. There's always a crowd in there, buying cigarettes, gossiping at the bar, hogging the phone. Lunch is catered in the villa but dinners happen each night in the restaurant over the road. Dani is in his element, holding court at the back table. He tips so lavishly that their table is always laden with delicacies, the owner joining for a grappa. He's the most local of everyone on the shoot, which in a funny way makes him the host, filling up glasses, spooning *osso buco* on to people's plates.

If Pasolini comes at all he comes in late, sits to one side, ironing out the day head to head with Dante, Dani, the head cameraman. People wait their turn, or bring their worries instead to the AD, who sits like a confessor, his face impassive, dispensing workarounds instead of Hail Marys. Then the Alfa is gone and so is Rocco. Nicholas feels deflation as sharp as if he had just ridden over a nail, and is unable to work out why it bothers him so much.

On a pink morning, waking with Dani beside him, he can smell spring coming. They're almost at the equinox, when night and day become equal. The trees are unfurling, each day the fields are softer and more richly green. But by nine he can't see further than his outstretched hand. It's freezing in the pig shed, despite the heater, and the libertines are surly as they are buttoned into their dresses. Today is the drag wedding, the most complicated scene from a costume point of view. None of them, it turns out, can walk in heels. They trip up and down the path, learning how to get their balance. For fuck's sake, Dani says, and puts on Uberto's pair. He sashays, pivots, returns. Use your hips, he tells them. Heel down first. Figure it out or we'll leave you in your regular shoes. Which might not be a bad idea.

Is there anything you can't do, Nicholas asks when he comes back in. Make you smile, Dani says, and then, as Nicholas grins – nope, I can do absolutely everything.

Only Giorgio is not wearing drag. As a bishop, the representative of religious power, he wears instead one of the weirdest costumes Dani has ever made. A golden yoke is set across his shoulders, with stylized ram heads protruding from either end. Gauzy red fabric hangs down from it, creating a parody of liturgical dress. On his head is a heavy silver crown, decked with lacquered oak leaves. On either side Dani has welded mirrored squares that hang down to his chest like grotesque pendant earrings, vaguely Egyptian. He looks terrifying, in part because he is so out of place among the meticulously dated realism of everyone else's clothes.

Paolo is helped into his robes, a black corsage pinned to his shoulder. He wears a beaded choker. He has an unusually still face, exuding menace even when he's out of character. Where's my future husband, he asks now. I want to check he has the biggest dick. Dani sets a spotted veil over his face and fluffs it. Don't be greedy, he says. He's never liked Paolo.

The dicks are another of Sergio's inventions. They have been wildly popular on set. People wear them to the restaurant, or leave them in each other's beds. Each one is so big that the actor's own equipment can be stored in a single testicle.

Now the children have to be put into their Sunday best. The girls are tucked and buttoned into their cream and pink and mouse-grey dresses, the boys smoothed into school suits with shorts and grey socks. A lot of spots because a lot of chocolate, Dani says. At least stop eating it when you don't have to. Get to make-up, all of you. Bruno, pull up your socks. Right to the knee please. Renata, don't forget your clips!

The courtesans arrive from make-up just as the children leave. Their eyebrows have been plucked into non-existence, redrawn as single arcing pencil lines. They shimmy efficiently into their suits, crane their necks so Dani can deck them with jewels. Like attending to swans, he says. I thank you ladies for your professionalism. Sonia the pianist bows, her loose red hair and sorrowful face setting her apart from the hard blonde trio of courtesans.

The first take is chaotic. There are so many people to marshal. Pasolini is not angry or anxious. He never shouts.

He seems to know exactly how each frame should look, holding on to his impatience until it is achieved exactly and then racing on. It's as if the film lives inside him. They aren't creating it here, only standing by, so many midwives to its emergence.

Lean against the wall, Pasolini says now to the bridegrooms, the four guards known for obvious reasons as the fuckers. They are the rightful beneficiaries of Sergio's appendages. They're older than the victims, more manly, each of them unusually handsome. Like hustlers, please, Pasolini says. Lazy, at your ease. Guido, you have cigarettes? I think it would be nice for one of you to smoke. Lazy, lazy, no rush, no anxiety. How do hustlers stand, Giuseppe asks, and everyone laughs. Exactly like you.

Paolo is required to harangue the children before the wedding begins. He calls them parasites, he demands that they smile. They cower from him, then ruin the take by laughing. Again, again. Then Sonia, who today is playing an accordion instead of her piano, sets the instrument down and performs with Hélène a scene borrowed from a French film they were both in, a device Pasolini refers to as *contamination*. Its purpose is to cheer the children up. It requires them to scream, one in pain and the other mockingly, until they both break into hysterical laughter. They stand in front of the double mirrors, two figures reduplicated into infinity, screaming and laughing, screaming and laughing until the lunch bell goes and they are freed.

29

Everyone else might be unaffected, mysteriously immune, but the daily descent into hell is getting to Nicholas. Things are becoming a bit too mixed. Ezio is shot, he holds his arm aloft in a resistance salute. A girl's throat is cut, the libertines display her corpse, curled on the floor beneath an altarpiece of the Madonna and Child. They fall down, they get up. Is anyone actually dead. Yes, his body says. Someone is actually dead.

The house isn't helping. Last year, at Cinecittà, he loved the disorientations of the set. Now, it's messing with his head. Different time-frames have been rammed together, they don't quite fit. The villa has deliberately not been furnished in fascist style. The deco furniture, the degenerate paintings: all this is meant to hint at the existence of previous occupants, wealthy, cultured, probably Jewish, removed to some unspecified location. You know where. Then he steps into the kitchen, and everyone's eating crisps and trading stories. Back to 1975.

It's so cold, too. When he comes in from the yard the mist follows him, seeping down corridors, pooling in corners. Yesterday, passing through the salon to rearrange Paolo's black dress, he saw Alan looking at him from one of the tall mirrors. Of course that's where he was. Now he flinches away from reflections, fearful of catching a waiting smile.

Okay so he isn't sleeping, maybe an hour or two a night. Okay so his hands shake, so that he has to brace himself before approaching a button, a zip. Okay so he's unravelling a bit, but they're not exactly here for long. Maybe he can leave Alan behind, imprisoned behind glass like a malign spirit, while he escapes, unimpeded, back to Rome. There must be some kind of binding spell.

30

The scenes in the house are almost finished. After Easter, they will move to other villas, to film exteriors, bedroom scenes, the selection process, before wrapping up with the bloody finale in a reconstructed courtyard at Cinecittà. All that is left to film here is the scene where the libertines' four daughters are placed in a tub of shit. Sergio has excelled himself. He has been driving for days around the province, buying up supplies. He has created a device with a hosepipe, through which he expels chocolate turds. This is a very clever innovation, Dani says to Nicholas as they watch. Sergio is a master illusionist. He isn't joking. Skilled, canny work thrills him, no matter how repellent the results.

The girls are placed in their barrel, their hands bound, a blue ribbon tied to each of their upper arms. Their make-up is exquisite. Chocolate is smeared on to their bodies, rubbed into their hair. There better be hot water today, Tatiana says. If I don't die of disgust I'll freeze to death. The fuckers are lounging against the wall again. This time, they play cards. That looks great. But stretch your legs out, Pasolini says. At your ease. Okay, so Tatiana, try this. Scream: God, why have you forsaken me? She looks at him disapprovingly. Isn't it blasphemous, she asks, to say Christ's own words on Good Friday? I think it might be a bit late to worry about that, Dani murmurs into Nicholas's ear.

After the scene is finished, the girls rush upstairs to wash. Okay, Pasolini says. He's smiling. I think we got everything we need. Sergio is supervising the transfer of the chocolate to the old farm midden. What a waste, Dani says. We should have baked a cake. Chocolate flavoured with Tatiana's feet.

The energy in the house has changed. At dinner that night, the conversation revolves around Easter plans. A break has been agreed: three days of liberty before the shoot resumes. Dani is going to his mother's and nearly everyone else is heading back to Rome. Imagine being warm, Hélène says. A caretaker is needed to stay on in the house, and to his own surprise Nicholas volunteers. He doesn't want to join anyone else's family festivities, not even Dani's. He doesn't want his own status as a foundling pressed upon him. A waif begging for scraps, it turns his stomach. He's fed up of pretending he's okay, steeling himself to pass as normal. Maybe what he really needs is to let go. To look Alan in the eye, to confront his losses, to say goodbye.

That's his plan, anyway. But on the final evening something seems to happen between Pasolini and Rocco. They were going to drive in the Alfa back to Rome, to spend the Sunday with Pasolini's mother. But instead, Rocco boards the bus, a stupid flight bag on his shoulder, though everyone knows a farmhouse outside Mantua is the full extent of his worldly travels. His face is even more sullen than usual. The bus pulls away. The cars leave. Dani lingers. Are you sure you won't come? Her lamb is good. Oh boy, and her *colomba*. I've never known anyone to like sweets as much as you, Nicholas says. He touches Dani's worried face. It's okay. I'm tired, I'm just going to sleep and draw. You don't need to worry about me. Dani puts on his shades against the weak sunlight. He kisses Nicholas. I love you, he says, for the first time. I'm only twenty miles away, you can call me if you change your mind. Then he too gets in the Jeep and drives away.

Now only the Alfa is left. Nicholas carries on sitting on the bench outside the pig shed, waiting for Pasolini to leave. A pear tree in the orchard has burst into blossom overnight. The light is everywhere at once, diffused by mist. The grass shines. Even the sky glows, like a clean white fleece. Pasolini comes out with his coffee in his hand. Tight jeans, tight denim shirt, a maroon cardigan with leather patches at the elbows. Just the homeless left, he says. Don't worry, I won't disturb you. I have an article to write.

31

Pasolini retires to his own room. Nicholas has the house to himself. He makes a sandwich, he eats it in the garden. The mist has almost burned away. There are buds on the wisteria that he hasn't noticed before, fat brown buds glazed with purple. He wants to draw the house before they leave, and so he drags a wheelbarrow round to the front and sets it in the long grass, handles down, turning it into an impromptu seat. Nothing has ever been so soothing to him as drawing, nothing has ever been so effective a way of dissolving his own personality, vaporizing the contents of his head. He is no longer a person dragged by time. He enters it through a secret door; he nestles there, hidden from view. His hand works across the paper. The covered balcony is a space that fascinates him. There are two portholes, two openings on either side of the dainty stone arch in the middle of the balcony, and they cast round sunspots on the shadowed wall behind. As the sun rises, the circles slide imperceptibly down the wall. The earth is steaming. He can smell rotting figs, the occasional sweetness of pear blossom, hear the clatter of Pasolini's typewriter from an upstairs room. The sky, for the first time, is blue, not white, not grey. He breathes low in his chest, his blood travels through his body. At work, he is a calm animal.

It's the absence of sun that rouses him. The house is just a house, no longer complicated by light. He's so cold he's shivering. He jumps up, and as he does he sees a little green snake, barred with black. His cry brings Pasolini to the window. It's nothing, it's nothing, he calls. I'm not afraid, I was just startled. Just a grass snake. It's gone already.

Back inside, he makes a coffee, warms his hands on the cup. He could have a bath, he could go to sleep. Instead, he decides to cook. Unlike Dani, he is not a natural cook, but there is something about the rhythm of chopping carrots, onions, potatoes that soothes him further. He is only making stew, the sort of thing he lived off as a student in London. He fries beef he finds in the fridge, scrapes it into the pan. Is that the wrong way round? He can't remember. He feels the fiercest longing for Dani, can almost hear his sardonic, amused voice. Oh good, cat food. Ivy around an oak, that's him.

It's dusk. He curls himself on a rocking chair in the kitchen, listens to the stew bubbling quietly. An owl hoots outside. He puts on his coat, he stands in the yard. No moon. Constellations like pinpricks in velvet. He tries to match them up in his head, but the only ones he can remember are Orion the hunter and Cassiopeia, the queen imprisoned on her terrifying chair. He remembers the painted ceiling he saw with Dani in Mantua, the cheerful little dog, the falling boy. Imagine being so lost you only had stars to rely on. He goes back in and bolts the door.

To his surprise, Pasolini appears as he starts to serve himself stew. He sniffs appreciatively, finds himself a bowl, a spoon. Is it okay, he asks. Do you mind sharing? Nicholas does not mind sharing. They eat in the kitchen. It is the first time they have been alone together since the trip to Villa Feltrinelli three months earlier. Nicholas asks the questions that have accumulated over the past few weeks. What do you mean by contamination? Why do you not control the actors' faces? He is asking about realism, he realizes, asking why Pasolini is so determined to sabotage its conventions. Because it's wrong, Pasolini says. It is imprecise and it is false. He stretches back expansively. Do you know, he says, I think I would like a grappa. Shall we take our drinks into the salon, as if we too were libertines?

They light the fire. They drink. Pasolini explains something of his theory of the montage versus the long shot. The montage is subjectivity, provisionality; the long shot is objectivity, clarity, resolution. The montage is the disorder of life; the long shot is the clarity of death. Which is true though? Which best represents reality? Nicholas is not quite sober. The lack of sleep has removed some of his defences, his capacity to withstand alcohol. He looks at their two bodies, reflected back and forth, back and forth, in the double mirrors. I once lived in a mirrored room, he says. I lived with a man who was married, and he made an apartment where he could keep me, and he decorated it so that it was an exact replica of his room at home. Every detail. Even the books. Even the carpet.

Pasolini is crouching on the floor, arms wrapped around his knees, gazing into the fire. He might not be listening. I didn't know at first, Nicholas says. And then I found out. Well, did you mind? Pasolini asks in his soft voice. Yes. I did mind. It made me feel like a doll. It made me feel like I wasn't quite real. Nicholas lies back, watches the red-haired boy in the mirror copy him limb for limb. He was a powerful person, a politician. I wanted to get away and so I – He founders here, uncertain what word to use. I suggested it would be sensible if he gave me money. I didn't blackmail him. Blackmail, he looks at Pasolini, blackmail means that you write a letter. I never wrote it down. And what happened in this story, Pasolini asks. He is still gazing into the fire, he hasn't looked at Nicholas once. He. He hiccups. Alan. He killed himself. I don't know. I didn't know he was scared. I just wanted to – He can't speak. He has already said far more than he meant to.

There is silence in the mirrored room. Nothing happens. Nothing is said. Nicholas can hear himself breathing. And then, still without looking at him, Pasolini lays a hand, unambiguously, on his leg.

32

He wakes the next morning in his own bed. There are people in the house. He listens to unfamiliar voices. He can't pinpoint them. Has someone come back? He pulls on jeans and a sweater, lopes down. There in the kitchen is Ninetto and his wife Patrizia. She is holding a baby. The older boy, Pier Paolo, is struggling in Pasolini's arms. Happy Easter, kid, Ninetto says. We brought cakes. We thought this one was getting lonely up here so we came to take him out for lunch. Nico holds his hands up. No need to include me, he's about to say, but there is no evading this storm of hospitality. He's given the baby, he's poured coffee, he's handed a slice of cake. *Pasqua, Pasqua*, the little boy chants. Nicholas consumes the offerings and excuses himself to find a clean shirt.

He can't begin to process the night. He has the unpleasant sense that part of his interior has escaped and is walking around on its own. He actually looks down at his hands, worried for a moment that he has become transparent, that his bones are visible. It's okay, surely. The talking cure: maybe that was the binding spell he needed. He looks surreptitiously at the mirror as he passes. No Alan. Just his own white face. He forces a smile. Happy Easter, kid.

33

Dani returns on Monday. He is rested, he looks sleek as an otter, his good coat loose, his sunglasses on. He jumps out of the car, grabs Nicholas in his arms. I bet you didn't eat a single thing, he says. Well you guessed wrong! I cooked a stew. I thought about saving you some but I knew you'd criticize how I cut the potatoes. A look of genuine pain crosses Dani's face.

The plan is that everyone will reconvene tomorrow in a new villa in Cavriana, north of Mantua, in which Dante has created an assortment of bedrooms and parlours. After that, they will travel to the Villa Aldini, a big ugly place outside Bologna that has been chosen to serve as the exterior, the façade of de Sade's Silling. They'll finish up with a day at Villa Sorra, just outside Modena, filming the last selection scenes. And then, says Dani, back to Cinecittà, where we will remain imprisoned for the rest of our natural lives. *Casanova* starts the minute we wrap. God knows when we get an actual holiday, and he cracks his fingers with pleasure at the work ahead.

Before they can leave, they have to pack up the pigsty, ensuring each costume is labelled and zipped into its plastic shroud. The shoes and hats are boxed, everything is ready to be loaded on to the truck. I'll tell you something I don't understand, Nicholas says, as they walk together into the house to pick up his bag. If all the interiors are in different places, how will it fit together? I mean, if Paolo walks out of a door in this house, how do you make sure it makes sense when he appears in the garden of another? Oh my God, says Dani, what do you think my job is? What do you think the girl with the Polaroid camera is doing? We have to match it all. It's like playing chess, it gets harder and harder as you go along. No, says Nicholas, but what I mean is, what if the light is wrong? What if it's raining? What if someone forgets their earrings? Someone is me, says Dani. And someone doesn't forget anything, ever. And someone is also Pasolini, and you know I think he remembers every scene he has ever shot, every word he has ever heard spoken on a set. He's got a perfect memory. After that, Nicholas doesn't ask any more questions about continuity.

He runs up to their bedroom to grab his duffle bag. Now he's leaving, he feels a little wistful about the house. The builders are already in the salon, unscrewing the lights, taking down the mirrors. They might never hang opposite each other again. A channel opened, and now it's sealed.

On the drive north he is merry and so is Dani. They sing along to the radio, they tease each other. It's very strange, Dani says, but we have barely been apart from each other since we met. And I missed you! I didn't even appreciate my solitude! I didn't realize when I picked up the lost boy on the street that I'd be keeping him so long. I wasn't lost,

Nicholas says. I was in transit. It's not the same. I really, really want you to fuck me, he adds abruptly, and Dani stops the car on a long green Lombardy road. He takes Nicholas's throat in one hand, caressing it, feeding his fingers into Nicholas's open mouth. Greedy boy, he says. Pull down your jeans and ask me again. Nicely.

34

The new villa is far grander than the last, an actual sixteenth-century palazzo where Napoleon III is supposed to have stayed. They pass through an arch in a cream wall, into a neglected garden dominated by cypresses and cedars, the immoderate purple of an unchecked wisteria. The story going around is that the present owner was so deeply in debt the whole estate was requisitioned by the bank just after Christmas. This is why the house is empty, its staff dismissed, its furniture sold off.

This is also why they've been given so much licence to reinvent it. Dante has been busy, yanking up floorboards, smashing in doors. He takes them on a tour. The half of the house in which everyone is staying is tidy and spartan. No Napoleonic bed though. Entering the other half is like going from peacetime to war. It looks as if it has passed through repeated cycles of abandonment, looting, requisitioning, as if the owners are all dead, as if soldiers have camped here and interrogations have taken place in every room. The wallpaper is peeling. Dani looks at it. It has a stylized pattern of green and blue fleur-de-lis. I know where you bought that, he says. And now I know where my costume budget went, too. He is particularly impressed by the faded patches on the wall, meant to imply missing paintings. What did you use? Touch it, says Dante, laughing. I did it by puffing flour through a cardboard frame.

This is just to impress you. I'll have to do it again tomorrow. I can't find the fixative. God forgive anyone who sneezes.

Part of the complexity of the design is that the villa is providing interiors for more than one location. It will serve both as the house where the female victims are selected, and as the upstairs rooms in the villa where they end up. The continuity is complicated. Dante shows them the retiring room he has made for the libertines. It is filled with Futurist and Cubist paintings: skilful copies of Juan Gris and Giacomo Balla. One wall is covered in a mural. Léger, Dani says. In his suicidal period. Look at those colours. If set design doesn't work out you could be a forger. Then he looks closer. You didn't make these. I know who made these! Dante laughs. I had no choice, he says, holding his palms up appeasingly. We were in a hurry. I requisitioned your workshop at Cinecittà. They said they didn't have much on, and with this inflammatory comment he hurries from the room.

All afternoon buses and trucks draw up. The kids are excited to be back, running in and out of each other's dormitories. Dani patrols the room at dinner, checking, he says, on who has eaten too much *colomba* over Easter. Hélène appears with a cushion under her suit. Dani, she says, in heavily accented Italian, you will have to make me a whole new wardrobe by tomorrow.

They start with the selection sequence. Girls in their uniforms sit huddled on the floor in the fleur-de-lis room.

There are picture frames stacked on the floor, packing cases, an atmosphere of desolation. More girls stand in the corridor outside. The libertines are in a salon downstairs, lounging on a coral-coloured corner sofa. The prettiest are brought down by extras playing procurers. The men look like black marketeers, the women like màdams in a whorehouse. One by one, the girls are displayed, undressed, their assets considered. One is rejected because of a missing tooth. Symmetry, Nicholas thinks, is the dominant attribute of beauty under fascism. Individuality, heterogeneity is not tolerable. Outside, it has begun to drizzle. It is difficult to shoot in the stairwell with the reduced light and an entire afternoon is wasted trying to get a shot of two girls crossing on the stairs.

In the break, Nicholas goes outside, standing under the portico. He wonders, not for the first time, if he should start smoking. Just for something to do. The rain has stopped. After something happens you feel as if something is about to happen but the fact is the thing has already happened. He has noticed this before. Why is he so full of anticipation. He imagines pouring water over the ashes of a fire. The sound a faint hissing.

35

Uberto is sitting on the floor, leaning against a chaise longue, his legs stretched out before him. The other libertines are in chairs, slouching with their drinks, as if it is very late at night. The lamps are lit, there are bottles open on the table. They are alone and untended. The principle, says Pasolini. The principle, says Uberto, of all greatness has long been totally bathed in blood. No, no, says Pasolini. The principle of all greatness on the earth. Okay, says Uberto. He drinks from his glass. The principle of all greatness on the earth has long been totally bathed in blood. And, my friends, if my memory does not betray me – yes, that's it: without bloodshed, there is no forgiveness. Without bloodshed. Baudelaire. Uberto looks at Pasolini. I don't think I should say that. As a writer. I don't think it looks good to misquote Baudelaire. My friend, Pasolini says, we are demonstrating that facts are immaterial in fascism, that truth is dead, that meaning is on a permanent migration. I think we are engaged in honourable work. Will you set aside your reputation for the cause? Uberto does not like to be laughed at. He steals another quick sip of his drink. I don't want to say it, he says. Okay, says Pasolini. That's okay. Aldo, you say the line. And Uberto, when he finishes, you can correct him. Say it's not Baudelaire, it's Nietzsche. But it's not Nietzsche, says Uberto. My dear friend, says Pasolini, might I remind you that we're acting?

36

There are currently four possible endings to the film. They are trying the first today. It will take place in the libertines' study after the killing spree is complete. Two of the boy guards have been left behind, forgotten, perhaps, rather than deliberately spared. What Pasolini wants is for them to dance together, clumsily, while 'These Foolish Things' plays on a radio. It is important that the actual song is playing while they film, even though it will be dubbed in later, and so Nicholas's job is to turn it on each time Rocco twiddles the dial. The boys are meant to be a little awkward, but neither of them knows what a foxtrot is. Okay, says Pasolini. Nicholas, start it up again. *Ba ba ba da ba*, Pasolini sings to himself as he dances in a neat circle. Come here Nico, he says, and Nicholas finds himself folded once again into a tight, impersonal embrace. He smells gum and cologne, and underneath a pungent scent that sets off a storm of arousal in his own body. He steps through three revolutions of a foxtrot and is set firmly aside. He holds himself like a soldier, trying to keep control, trying not to gasp out loud, the blood rising in his face.

37

Does it matter, Dani thinks. Does it change anything? What, the boy is fuckstruck, temporarily in orbit around the largest planet in the solar system. He sensed it the minute he got out of the car, sensed it maybe back in Salò at the end of last year. All those nasty comments Nicholas kept making; he'd talked exactly like that about people he desired. You come on set, you have a thing with the director, so what? It opens things up again, which is after all his own natural state. Maybe it was these weeks, twined around each other, that were the aberration. Time to step back.

38

The second ending no one likes. They film it at Villa Aldini a week later, after they have completed the arrival scene, the libertines on the balcony reading out their apocalyptic laws to the bewildered children on the grass. Again, it is supposed to take place after the terrible bout of murders, the killing spree they will film next month at Cinecittà, in a studio Dante is even now turning into a sinister courtyard, with fake brick walls and a sand floor, set out at intervals with wooden pegs.

In this version of the ending, the scarlet banners of the Italian Communist Party are unfurled from the villa's windows. Oh no, Pasolini says, watching it through the camera's eye. Oh no, that won't do at all.

39

The third ending is planned but also spontaneous. It is also filmed at Villa Aldini. Everyone is in it. It is like the end of *8½*. The cast come out of the house, on to the lawn. They run around, a little clumsily at first. They dance, they romp. The crew come out and join them. Dante, Danilo, Sergio are all there. Pasolini runs in, still holding the Arriflex on his shoulder. Hélène and Paolo dance, people link hands, torturers with victims, actors with caterers and electricians. The garden is surrounded by a circular yew hedge. It is set on a hill above Bologna, so when the camera steps back the people are dancing above that rose-red city. The dead are risen, the harm is undone. Perhaps it is too good to be true, perhaps it undermines the desolations that precede it. Cut.

ACT 3

PIOMBO

1

Rome is a basket of flowers, Rome is an oven. Danilo spent May in the demonic courtyard in Studio 15. His final costumes for *Salò* were black underpants, with holsters for knives. It was Sergio who excelled himself in those final weeks, creating false breasts, testicles, nipples, scalps, stomachs, tongues. I want to show what power does to the human body. It's basically the annulment of the personality of 'the other', Pasolini tells a journalist. The sand is sticky with red paint.

Now it is June, and Danilo is back in his own womblike workshop in Studio 16. Was it an exorcism, after all, or an invitation? Normally he can shake a film off but *Salò* stays with him, even though he has so far declined invitations to view the footage, to watch the edit as it progresses. What the film means to him is that the past is not past, that there is a porosity to time that talk of historic eras, discrete moments succeeding one another, can only imperfectly conceal. This age, that age, the war, the economic miracle. *Salò* is a new account of time, the perpetual wounding present of *I will take*. It makes Danilo feel ill, it makes his life, his patiently accumulated days, look worse than blinkered. Why do you run so fast, if what you have to say is so pessimistic, he once asked Pasolini, and in response, the sweetest smile. Because I am still burdened by the emergency of hope.

This mood is leaking into *Casanova*, he can't help it. Everything disgusting, nothing redeemed. To fuck is to conquer, what a terrible thing to think. And yet a part of him recognizes the ubiquity of the charge. Once, years ago, Pasolini confided in him a dream he'd had about Ninetto that made him realize – the phrase has stuck – *what my ambiguous love of liberty was against*. What is his ambiguous love of liberty against? Boredom, convention, stasis. Or love, the cuckoo in his bed.

He needs to ask Nicholas to move out. He should ask Nicholas to move out. He wants to ask Nicholas to move out and then they wake up, bodies tumbled together, already laughing at something. What life does he want? He has barely seen Piero this year. There is ground to make up there. He tries to see Nicholas objectively, to picture him as a stranger. It's not possible. Long legs, red hair, who cares. Even the perfection of his face is irrelevant. It's the way he opens himself, the way his pupils widen as Dani undoes his belt. He's so responsive, so mercurial, it's so easy to make him laugh, so easy to have him gasping on the floor. The fact is that Dani has never wanted anyone so much, not since he was a teenager himself. But he needs his house back. He needs to draw a circle around himself, he needs – okay, whatever, it's true – not to be left high and dry, flat on his ass, wrecked by a kid. The truth glimpsed in the doorway in Cavriana is that he is in danger, that he has gambled more than he can afford. It is not the kind of danger he enjoys.

He will speak, he tells himself. He will do it when he gets home. Nothing major, no drama, no rupture. He still wants to see the kid. Just not such a watertight world, a universe of two.

He takes the tram back to the city. It is a luminous evening, rippled with pink. He gets the bus through the Borghese gardens and walks from Flaminio, stopping by the river to see a boat crossing the reflected sky. The lights are on when he lets himself into the building, and he can hear Nicholas singing to himself as he opens the door. There are candles on the table, a bottle of champagne. What's all this, he asks. I got pork chops too, Nicholas says, but I thought it was better if I didn't cook them. It's my birthday actually and I realized – Wait, sit down first.

He opens the champagne, clumsily, using his shirt. I didn't know it was your birthday, Nico. I would have bought you something. You shouldn't be buying your own dinner. No, listen, Nicholas says. *Cin-cin*. He raises a foaming glass. I just wanted to say, I'm twenty-three now, and this is the first birthday where I've felt like I had a real home. I mean a home with someone who didn't want me to be someone else. I don't – A blush has engulfed him. Dani, you make everything good. I've never known anyone who could do that. I just wanted to say thank you. He takes a sip, the tips of his ears burning.

Dani drinks. He cooks the chops. He loves the boy. Perhaps it is inescapable. And even if he didn't, even if it wasn't, it is not within his nature to break this kind of pact.

2

He imagines himself as a diver. He puts on his helmet, he checks his oxygen tank. He climbs the steps and casts himself off, somersaulting backwards into the eighteenth century. He travels down, breathing audibly. There are rooms and then there are things. Candlesticks and clocks. A golden carriage. The most worn-out, exhausted and bloodless of all centuries, Fellini has called it, but to make this apparent the film must be overpopulated, thronged with wonders.

Today he is making a mirror, a magic mirror that will be on the wall in the Marquise d'Urfé's private chamber. He consults the *Encyclopédie de la Divination* that Fellini has given him. Inside is a photograph of a mirror, ornate, overwrought. *Comme une porte ouverte sur les allées d'un jardin enchanté*, the caption reads. He leans over the page with his magnifying glass, pulls the lamp closer. It must be ivory, the carving is so finely worked. The outer room of the workshop is full of people, but he has retreated to his inner sanctum, the kitchen. Stock is bubbling behind him. He sits at the table where he rolls pastry and sketches out a design to be cast in papier mâché and spray-painted gold. He is two things: a German craftsman in the sixteenth century and a bandit. He needs to know how it was made and to make it. Not the same.

3

Pasolini rang, Dani says. He keeps his voice deliberately neutral. He says call him. The number's by the phone.

Okay, Nicholas says.

He rings while Dani is cooking. He invited me to the house, he reports a few minutes later. Not chatty, is he.

The house is in the EUR, the neighbourhood designed during fascism. Nicholas has never been there before. It's like he's travelled into the future. The buildings are enormous, but there is no one on the streets. He passes a vast white stone cube composed of row after row of arches, six by nine, like a beehive. Its regularity, its extreme featurelessness and inhuman scale conspire to make him feel small and dirty. He imagines it as an amplifier for a voice: a robotic voice that can only issue commands. Why would you choose to live here?

Pasolini's house is round the back of Santi Pietro e Paolo, on Via Eufrate. It is grander than Nicholas expected. Not grand: it is more moneyed than Nicholas expected. It is gated, there is an entry phone, a pleasant, not quite tame garden. My mother has gone to bed, Pasolini says. He makes tea, in cups that have a pattern of ivy leaves. Nicholas's own grandmother had a set just like them. There are newspapers on the table, a cut-glass bowl filled with oranges. How strange, that Pasolini is a boy who never left home, his typewriter set up in his mother's parlour.

They talk about the *Salò* edit. The film is being dubbed into French, not Italian. To assert its status as an intellectual work, Pasolini explains. Though it will no doubt be banned as pornography whatever I do. The sex is a metaphor, he adds. Did I say that already? Who gets fucked and how. It isn't literal.

It is almost midsummer, and the room faces directly west. Nicholas has to raise an arm to block out the last rays of sun. I'll close the shutters, says Pasolini, but already it is setting. He stands by the window, pointing out the Via Ostiense, once an ancient Roman road, now the SP8, and beyond it the Tiber. The sea is only fifteen miles from here, he says. You can smell it sometimes.

We could have cake, he suggests. He brings out a flat cake dusted with icing sugar. He cuts them damp slices that taste of walnuts.

I think I owe you something, he says at last. Nicholas is so horrified he half rises, physically pushing the suggestion away. Sit down, sit down. I'm not talking about sex. You told me a story, and I have a story too, which I think belongs alongside it. But I didn't say it, and I think that was wrong. He gets up again, and sits back down at the head of the table, at right angles to Nicholas. I had a brother. You know this?

Nicholas does not know.

I had a brother, Guido. A younger brother. Sweet, very handsome, not – I say this because it is important – not as clever as me. More normal.

Straight, Nicholas says.

Yes. But also, more normal. Not as dreamy. Not as ambitious. We were very close. He wore my clothes, my hand-me-downs. You know we lived in Friuli, in the north?

Again, Nicholas shakes his head.

Okay, so we lived in Friuli. My father was a prisoner of war in Africa. He was a fascist, a real believer, and my mother, Susanna – he indicates the door behind which she is presumably asleep – was not a fascist. She was an anti-fascist, in her way. She hated Mussolini. And the war started, and we were boys with mud in our ears, and it took until Mussolini was deposed to realize what we thought. And then we were anti-fascists too. But I was a poet first, and second I was a poet who wanted to make love, who wanted to walk in the meadows and look at the boys and write down what he felt. I boiled over into words. He looks at his hand. And into my hand too, he says and laughs, a little. Guido wasn't like that. His energy, his enthusiasm, it was all for the resistance. He wrote slogans on the walls in town, he almost got caught. He stole weapons from the Nazis, he distributed leaflets. It was so dangerous, you can't imagine. Then he decided to join the partisans. I went with him to the station. He was wearing my old jacket; it was already too small for him. I watched him walk away. That was the last thing I saw of him, the nape of his neck.

Ciao Ezio, Nicholas says, and Pasolini's head snaps up. Yes, exactly, he says. That scene in Roncoferraro, that soft-faced boy. That was Guido.

Okay, so he finds the partisans, up in the hills. He stays with them all winter. But there's a conflict between the different groups. Friuli, you know, it's right on the border. There's a trial, a fake trial, and some of his band are found guilty and sentenced to death. They shoot Guido, but he gets away. They find him, he's injured, they bring him back. I didn't hear it at the time. I didn't find out what had happened until the spring. They took him into the mountains and they laid him in a grave and then they shot him.

He looks at Nicholas. So both of us carry a body. That's all I wanted to say. I took your story and I didn't give one back.

The stories are not the same, but Nicholas doesn't say that. He understands that they are about guilt and queerness, about being the person who survives, who is condemned to spend the rest of their life throwing themselves again and again at the electric rail. The person who writes poems, chases boys, the alley cat, never not on trial. Pasolini is looking intently at the table. There is an inch of bare skin exposed between his socks and his trousers. Thank you, Nicholas says. He sets his fork on the plate. He lets himself out.

4

Then finally, Sutherland arrives. I had almost forgotten we were making a film, Dani says to Nicholas. I had started to believe I was in a dream, condemned to build palaces for the rest of my life. They are part of the welcome committee. Dani will be showing Sutherland the compressed Venice he has created around the pool. It is impressive, he knows it is: Santa Maria della Salute reflected in the murky waters of their own private Grand Canal. He awaits the group on the top of the Rialto Bridge, as Fellini has decreed. Nicholas, stealing a look, thinks he could not be more immaculate. Dani always seems more real than other people, his expensive shoes set firmly on the ground. Did the nuns make your scent, he asks, sniffing discreetly. You smell like a pharaoh. Look, they're coming.

Fellini is barrelling along at the centre of an entourage, his arms waving, indicating gondolas at the same time as he is evidently describing Casanova's wig. Sutherland walks peaceably beside him, in white jeans, his shirt open. He's wearing cowboy boots. I like his hair, Nicholas whispers. He looks very American, like he should be standing on a rock giving a sermon. Or shooting someone. Stop talking, Dani says crossly, without moving his lips, or I'll send you back inside. Anyway, he's Canadian.

And this, Fellini says, in his terrible English, is Danilo Donati, the greatest costume maker of the world. He is the magician who bring all this – he indicates St Mark's tower on his left, the basilica to his right – into life. Pleased to meet you, Sutherland says, offering a large manicured hand. Dani hates speaking English. After nine months with Nicholas he still refuses to say more than a handful of words he considers particularly ridiculous. Bobble hat. Suck my dick. Clearly neither will do now. *Pleased to meet you*, he repeats carefully, glaring at Sutherland. Nicholas, you better tell him he's too tall. We're going to need to remake all his breeches.

Instead, they escort Sutherland to the costume department, where a very small fraction of the *Casanova* costumes have been set up on mannequins. Now the actor comes to life. The polite smile peels off his face, he is as animated as a boy. So great, he murmurs. Absolutely. He indicates to Dani that he would like to try on the pink coat. They slip it over his shirt, tie the ribbons of a jabot at his neck. He consults the mirror, looking intently at his reflection. How fabulous, he says. Keep him on, keep him on, says Fellini. And now we go to make-up and I show you how we do your face. We work out how to make your eyes twice the size. Like a cow!

When they've left, Dani sits in the chair. He looks tired. I have a feeling, he says, that this is not going to be a happy shoot.

5

Three-quarters of Cinecittà has been consecrated to *Casanova*. Nicholas's current job is assisting in the painting department, where they are turning out Velázquez-style portraits of popes and princes, dukes and kings. Next door, Ettore and Vito are making a metal replica of Dürer's rhino, a ten-foot metal penis emerging from its back.

It's not an atmosphere in which to think, for which he is grateful, and yet he can't seem to stop himself from running through images. What he keeps seeing is the boy from *Salò*, Ezio, the soft-faced boy who alone among the guards didn't take to his brutal duties. In the end, he was caught in bed with a servant girl. When the libertines burst in, half-dressed, pistols drawn, he jumped up, stood naked by the bed and raised his fist in the communist salute. For a moment the men froze, then Paolo shot him. Pitiful, courageous, absurd. Of course it's Guido.

The paintings all have a ground of tarry Mars black. Maybe it's not the best job to be doing. The same face keeps emerging, the jack of diamonds, his cheekbones like knuckles. For fuck's sake Nico, Ettore yells from across the room. You're supposed to be good at painting. They're meant to be wearing wigs, not looking like the devil.

6

Do you want to go to Ostia, Nicholas shouts. It's Saturday morning, they are in the flat, Dani in his study, Nicholas in the hall. I'm going. There's a football game this afternoon. There's a football game, Dani says incredulously. What do you care about that? Pasolini rang, he suggested that we come. I've never been to Ostia. Wouldn't it be fun?

In the end, Nicholas goes alone, on the Vespa. Dani refuses. He turns himself inward, he hunches at his chair. Just go, he says. I have so much work to do, you can't imagine. And there is nothing I hate more than men kicking balls. You're sulking, Nicholas says, but Dani doesn't reply.

It's the hottest day of the summer so far. He's wearing cut-offs and plimsolls, an old shirt to stop his back from burning. Even with his sunglasses on the glare is painful. Light is bucking off the horizon. When did he last see the sea? In Venice, that day on the Lido, last September. He wishes Dani was with him, a conspiratorial non-participant. He doesn't like men kicking balls either. He was, let's face it, just ecstatic to be asked.

There are umbrella pines on the horizon. The land is opening out, becoming scrubby. It's not even really a road any more, just a dirt track between shacks and heaps of rubbish. The smell of piss and rotting garbage is oppressive.

There are kids playing with a dog on a chain. Playing. One of them lobs a stone at him. It ricochets off the scooter. He loves places like this, despite the stench, the sense of danger: on the edge, peripheral, between the land and the water. The Tiber is just out of sight. Someone told him there are Roman ruins nearby, a whole city hidden beneath the grass.

At last he finds the field. The Alfa, bikes, a crappy Fiat. It's all kids, Pasolini in their midst, in his vest and silky little shorts, his socks tugged up. For some reason, Nicholas was expecting a hero's welcome – you made it! You're here! – but in fact his presence is barely acknowledged. What he'd like to do is walk to the sea, find an ice cream, gossip with Dani. Instead he's running ineffectually after a pack of boys, one of whom kicks him deliberately in the side of his knee. You little cunt, Nicholas says, and plunges after the ball. He scratches him, probably not allowed, and for a moment he takes possession. What's he supposed to do? He kicks it, as hard as he can, in the direction of the goal, and to his amazement it soars in the air and lands at the back of the net. Triumph roars up in his throat. He's already looking round to see Pasolini's pleased, startled face when Rocco thumps him between the shoulders. You fucking faggot, he says, that's our goal. One–nil to them. And he spits on the ground, just between Nicholas's feet.

It was great, he tells Dani later. Really fun. The high glare of humiliation, the feeling of wrongness in his body, it's all too painful, too familiar. This is England, this is what he ran away from: the laughter of boys who know that he is never going to get what he so disgustingly, so shamelessly is unable not to want.

7

Sourness has crept on to the set. Summer sourness, like spoiled milk. Fellini's secretary has her car stolen. She replaces it and that car is stolen too. His driver Ludo has to have an operation, which means the necessary calmness of his morning commute is contaminated by the presence of a stranger. The drive to Cinecittà has always been Fellini's best time to think and talk, to turn over the problems of the film, and without it he is on an even shorter fuse.

Then the chief architect is rushed to hospital. He's fine, but a few days before filming there is a more serious accident. A carpenter is killed, crushed beneath a pile of wood. People start to talk about the curse of *Casanova*. The curse of daily life and a badly organized wood shop, Danilo replies. He takes the afternoon off to visit the man's wife, and fights with Fellini about it afterwards.

The shoot finally begins on 21 July, nearly a whole year since Danilo began his drawings. The first scene is Casanova's assignation with a nun on an island in the lagoon. Instead of using the pools that will serve as the Grand Canal and the Thames, Fellini has insisted they create an artificial lagoon in the studio out of black plastic. It takes two days to set it up to his and Dani's satisfaction. The island is tiny, its soil stuck with stems of maize. The carpenters have produced two wooden cut-outs, painted dark green, to indicate cypresses. Sutherland holds up his candle. The nun sits in her little boat, tugging at the oars. What's my motivation here, Sutherland actually says. Wetting your dick, says Fellini, and then in English, passions of the heart.

Now Casanova must row back through a wild storm. Sutherland stands patiently while they pour water over his head. His hair is wild, his white clothes drenched. He rows against the wind machine, through volleys of spray. Nicholas has snuck away from his painting to watch. I know you are a wizard, he whispers to Dani, but he is definitely rowing through a sea of inflating black bin bags. Does it matter? It's what Fellini wants, Dani says. He hasn't taken his sunglasses off for three days.

Now a second boat approaches, an extraordinary black boat with a winged lion at the prow. It is the chief of police, Messer Grande, in the service of the Venetian Inquisition. A voice hails Casanova, shouting against the wind. Giacomo Casanova! You are under arrest! Casanova rows frantically, the wind whipping his cloak. No, he shouts. Why? The two boats rock up and down. Then there is an almighty crack and Messer Grande's boat cleaves in two. Fuck the devil up his arse, Dani says succinctly.

Back to the carpentry shop. Take two.

8

Sutherland's make-up takes three hours each morning, just as Dani predicted months ago. Once it is finished, he can no longer move his face freely. He has been converted into a puppet, a big puppet, identical from every angle. He is still trying earnestly to find his way into *the role*. He has brought with him armfuls of documentation about Casanova's life and times. He reads about Voltaire and alchemy as his chin, his brow are laboriously remade. He has requested that his dressing room be decorated as a Venetian boudoir, which is why Danilo has been crawling around on the floor, trying to work out if he can fit in a daybed upholstered in plum-coloured velvet. He has also given Sutherland a replica of the strange mechanical bird they've made, borrowed from another drawing in the *Encyclopédie de la Divination*. Casanova carries it with him to every assignation. While he pumps away, the bird flaps its metal wings, a fornicator's metronome. Sutherland names it Frank.

Over the course of these interactions, Dani has discovered that Sutherland does understand Italian, though he can only speak a hesitant, hybrid version. He learned it over the long winter in Emilia, filming *Novecento* with Bertolucci. But he is adamant that Fellini is not to know. So please don't tell him, he says to Dani, as his eyebrows are glued taut with tiny strips of tape. I know I can trust you to keep my secret. He gazes at him in the mirror, out of wide blue eyes that can no longer blink. His forehead is enormous. With Mr Fellini, he says thoughtfully, I am going to need every advantage I can get.

9

It's worse than that. It's like watching an abusive marriage. Dani knows that Sutherland is tough. He's heard reports from friends who worked on *Novecento*. But the actor has never had the experience of being hated by a director before. It's not a battle of wills, it is one person refusing to accept the existence of another. Fellini alternates between humiliating Sutherland, bullying him through the megaphone, and ignoring him completely, cutting him dead, turning away when he approaches. He always demonstrates scenes for his actors, playing out every gesture, every movement, but with Sutherland he does it insolently, contemptuously, as if there is no way that the actor will be able to grasp even the simplest of his instructions. Because the film is mostly about seduction, what this boils down to is him showing Sutherland how to fuck. He watches him pump away and then he laughs openly. Donaldino, he shouts through the megaphone, I see you are a stranger to pussy. Can you do it as if you were an accomplished lover or must I come down there and show you myself? And Sutherland ducks his head, abashed, even though his girlfriend is widely regarded as the most beautiful woman on set.

After the lagoon, they have moved on to the London sequence. Dani can't help wondering whether the selection has been made simply because both scenes involve

Sutherland being drenched. Water is hard work for actors. Take after take, neck-deep in the pool, which has been coloured for the occasion a murky, septic brown. The sequence begins with Casanova dumped on the banks of the Thames by a cackling mother and daughter, from whom he has contracted a venereal disease. This, it transpires, is not the worst of it. The greatest tragedy of your life has befallen you, Casanova cries out as he stands alone on the empty street, surrounded by bags. Your steed has failed to answer the commands of your desires.

London has been reduced to a stretch of wet pavement. Two equestrian statues are distantly visible through fog. Faced with impotence, Casanova resolves to end his life. Ever the dandy, he chooses his finest clothes for his appointment with death, donning a sequinned jacket, a fur hat, a diamond bow tie, right there in the street. He climbs down to the shore and wades into the churning water. Fellini waits until he is waist-deep and then bellows through the megaphone. You're plodding, Donaldino. You need to walk a little faster. Get him dry, someone. We'll start it from the beginning, please.

In the end, Sutherland walks into the river twelve times. Each time, he declaims the same poem, perfectly. He does it lightly, he does it with gravitas, he makes it lilting and in the end he weeps. The fog machine stops working. Oh dear, Fellini says. Let's leave it for today. We'll try it again tomorrow.

10

After work, Nicholas goes to the EUR again. He puts himself in Pasolini's path, even though it is clear that he is not wanted in the way that he wants to be wanted. Is it the not wanting that is the source of the attraction. He feels dull inside, he feels so hungry that he is ashamed. I told you, he wants to say. I gave my story to you, and you gave your story to me. This exchange, so heavily freighted with intimacy and risk: it should have been the beginning of something, but instead it was a blind alley, a dead end. The boys Pasolini chases are all the same. They are the same boy, infinitely reproduced. Perhaps there was an original once, up in the hills. Pockmarked, slim-hipped, cunning, poor. The intensity of his own obsession frightens Nicholas. He can't check it. He rings the buzzer, makes up a limp excuse.

This time, Pasolini sits him on the sofa. He is, he says, correcting poems. Is Nicholas interested? Might he in fact be interested in translating some of them into English? He would, he says, yes he says, nodding like a dog. Pasolini hands over a sheaf of paper. He smiles his soft impersonal smile.

Back in the flat, Nicholas looks them over. Sex is a pretext. Anoints with seed and then departs. A boy in his first loves is nothing less than the world's fecundity. He doesn't want to be a scrying glass through which the universe is glimpsed. He wants to be seen for what he is.

11

What saves Casanova from suicide is a vision of a giantess glimpsed through fog on the opposite bank. The giantess is called Sandy Allen. She's twenty-five, from Shelbyville, Indiana, and very shy. Last time Nicholas was in Studio 15 it was the courtyard from *Salò*. Today it has been transformed into the site of a travelling fair. There is mud on the ground, and mist hangs heavy in the air.

For weeks, Dani has been refining the set. Among the attractions is a swing carousel. It's pulled by a pony, always a nightmare in a studio. The idea is that three girls sit on the other side, their big skirts flying. Nicholas watches as the extras are funnelled through costume and make-up. He helps the giantess's miniature attendants, identical twin brothers, into their white wigs and scarlet coats. A contortionist hired from a circus is painting a grotesque face on to his abdomen. He makes the eyes roll, the lips move, and the extras scream their appreciation. A make-up girl is standing on a stepladder, dusting sequins on to Sandy Allen's forehead. There are fairground barkers and off-duty soldiers, all the dregs of eighteenth-century London. You should feel at home, Nico, Ettore says. These are your people, no?

Actually the presence of so many English is freaking Nicholas out. He has a terror of bumping into someone he knows. He sticks with Sandy, escorting her personally into Dani's pride and joy, the tent shaped like a whale. It is just like the sketch he made the morning that Fellini attacked the set: a melancholy whale with its great head raised, firelight illuminating its tiny startled eye. Wooden steps lead into its papier-mâché throat. Up go the Englishmen in their cocked hats, their giant cuffs. Up goes Casanova, hunting for marvels.

12

Sex has stopped. It's like Dani has exited his body, or travelled very deep into his own interior. Nicholas touches him, and he rolls up like a porcupine. He makes their coffee, but he doesn't sing or ruffle Nicholas's hair as he passes by. Nicholas thinks about saying something, but can't think what it would be. The dance between them has gone awry.

They travel to work separately, they come home at different times. One night, in early August, Nicholas lets himself in and senses a presence. I'm home, he shouts. I'm going to shower. Okay, says an unfamiliar voice. He walks into the kitchen, and there is Pinocchio with his shirt off, eating a doughnut filled with custard. Hi, Nicholas says uncertainly. Are you looking for Dani? I don't think he's here. He's at Fagiani, Pinocchio says. I just left him there. We got one for you too but I ate it. He grins unrepentantly, crumbs on his face. I'm staying a while. I guess Danilo forgot to say.

Are you fucking kidding me, Nicholas says three minutes later. They're in the bedroom. I don't want him here. He's trying to keep his voice low. I'm sorry Dani, I don't like him. This is my flat, Danilo says. The kid's in trouble. I said he could have a bed. What bed? What bed? We have one bed. Calm down Nicholas. He can sleep on the sofa. For how long, Nicholas asks. I don't know, Dani says. For as long as he needs. He works for me and he hasn't got anywhere to sleep. What do you suggest I do?

The entire conversation would be different if Dani were smiling, but he looks at Nico like a stranger, like a stranger he dislikes. I thought you'd be more understanding, he says. Since you have also needed rescuing. It's not a statement that can be unsaid. It lies between them, leeching its poison. And I brought nothing with me, Nicholas says. So it will be easy to pack.

13

Panic is flaring through his system, panic and rage. He throws his clothes into his bag, leaves his coat on its hook, it's summer, who cares. Danilo does not try to stop him. It's pathetic how little he has.

His heart is still racing when he reaches the river. Where to go, what to do? It's evening, the stone is glowing. The air is warm on his skin. He isn't hungry, he isn't tired. The best place would be Ettore's, but he can't remember the address. It's somewhere in San Lorenzo. He could walk over there, ask around. In his rush he has forgotten the existence of the Vespa. The keys are in his pocket, but he can't bring himself to go back to Dani's street. Obviously he could go to Pasolini's, get the subway to the EUR, press the buzzer, listen for the click as the gate is released. And then what, beg a night on the sofa, like all the little delinquents who come bearing hard-luck stories. I need to hide from the cops, Pà, I've run away from my dad. He watches the junk floating by, a nest of twigs, the corpse of a fat rat. It's summer. Better to spend the night outdoors and find Ettore in the morning.

He doesn't want to be on the streets and so he stays on the riverbank, following the Tiber through its loops, dodging partygoers and courting couples. The starlings are settling in the plane trees. They are always so disputatious at dusk.

He walks and he walks, and at three or four he curls up in a park, he doesn't know its name, his bag clutched in both arms. He doesn't sleep. He lies on the earth and waits for morning. Above his head the sky passes from black to blue to pink.

It's not until the sun is up that he realizes he won't see Ettore at work since he presumably no longer works for Dani. He isn't thinking right. There is too much turmoil inside him, it's like he's been hit in the face. He brushes leaves from his body, he sets off again. Ettore is a creature of habit. If Nico waits at the bottom of Via Tiburtina he'll catch him on his way to work. At seven he is at the café on the corner, nursing a coffee, just in case, but Ettore doesn't appear until eight fifteen. What the fuck happened to you, he says, clapping Nicholas on the arm. You look rough. Did you sleep in a ditch? He listens to the story, he sucks his teeth in sympathy. To be fair, Nico, that kid was there before you. And no, I don't like him either. He thinks, he eats the *cornetto* Nicholas buys him. Are you coming to work, he asks. Maybe best not, today. I can see how it is when I get in. I mean, you could stay with me but there's a lot of us at home. But I can talk to my cousin. He might have a better idea.

Ettore's cousin also works at Cinecittà. He's older, and has never struck Nicholas as friendly. Great, he says. He makes himself smile. Thanks, buddy. I'll meet you back here tonight? Ettore rolls his eyes. I mean, I'll see you in a bar. You can buy me a beer. He scribbles a name on a grubby scrap of paper he finds in his pocket. There, or the next one along. Opposite the station. They have pinball machines, you can entertain yourself if I'm late.

It's a long time since he's had a day to waste. Work keeps him anchored, being busy stabilizes his thoughts. Left to his own devices, he is assailed by paranoia. Is he walking strangely. Is this the right way to cross a road. He doesn't want to check into a hotel. If he no longer has a job, he needs to conserve his money. He's near the cemetery, but that doesn't feel like a good place to go. Instead he takes the bus up to the Borghese gardens, buys a bag of peaches and a roll and spends the day falling in and out of sleep under the shadow of the trees. Each time he wakes it is with his heart going hard in his chest. Eat a peach, watch the dogs, throw the pit down for the ants. Later, he has a Coke in a café, uses the bathroom, checks himself in the narrow mirror. His hair is dark with sweat. There are tiny bumps all over his forehead, his cheeks. One day on his own and he's falling to pieces. He splashes water on his face, resists the urge to slap himself.

Ettore is late. Nicholas has stationed himself outside, so he can watch both sides of the street. It's a boy bar, like most of the places in front of the station. Hustlers, none of them exactly professional. The owner tolerates the kids, doesn't mind if they keep a single espresso going all afternoon. Nicholas watches a pinball game out of the corner of his eye. One of the boys watching is also dealing. Embrace, back slap, and the notes slide into his back pocket. He's good, he never fumbles. Scarlet shirt with a big collar, tight blue jeans, ankle boots. Curly hair escaping a badly made quiff. He feels Nicholas looking, turns his eyes but not his face. Yes?

Ettore sits down heavily. After all that, Nicholas didn't even see him coming. Hey, he says. How does it feel to be unemployed? Because guess what, you're not. Danilo was going crazy that you weren't there. They're so behind, you better be back tomorrow. Nicholas frowns. Okay, he says. And I found you a place too, so you can get me that beer. I've been a good friend to you today. My cousin says you can borrow his room, no problem, he's going away this week. But he wants to ask you a little favour in return.

The little favour is very simple. Fredo works as a technician at Cinecittà and one of his jobs is to drop the reels of negatives each night at the Technicolor lab on Via Tiburtina. But he has to go away tonight, Ettore says, and he wondered if you could run them up. Sure, says Nico. No problem. But I left the Vespa in Prati. How late is it open? Oh no, it's easier than that, Ettore says. Fredo is coming here on his scooter. You can borrow it and bring it straight back. If he can wait for it why doesn't he go himself, Nico thinks but doesn't say. A ride for a bed is a good exchange.

Fredo arrives, he sits on his scooter, talking mainly to Ettore. They're Neapolitan, it's a different language, Nico can't quite keep up. So, Ettore says, turning back to him, the important thing is that you wear the helmet, so nobody knows you aren't him. He's worried about his job. The whole thing is sounding more and more crazy. It's hot, the beer is sour in his stomach. Sure, Nico says again. Give me the keys.

He's never seen a film can before. It's a flat silver disc the size of a pizza, with a bright green label, heavier than he expected. Via Tiburtina 1138, he reads. Yes, says Fredo in his flat voice. They buzz you in, you show my pass, they take you through to the store. The same numbers are on the side of the can and on the shelf. You find the number, and then you just put it down with the others. That's it. Nothing to it. His smile is also flat. Don't fuck up my scooter. I'll leave my room key with Ettore. I gotta go now.

He's right. There is nothing to it. Nicholas rides the unfamiliar scooter to the outskirts of the city. Warehouses, shacks, open fields. The Technicolor lab is a long grey building with small windows. He keeps the helmet on, he shows his pass. He is taken down a corridor, and through a heavy set of doors into the vault. It is noticeably colder. There must be thousands of films in here, stacked floor to ceiling in their silver cans. He works his way down the shelves until he reaches 8299. It's like navigating in an unfamiliar library. *Casanova* is next to *Salò*. So the order is chronological, not alphabetical. He sets the can in its rightful place. Thanks, he says to the receptionist and steps out into the diminishing heat of the evening.

That scooter, he says to Ettore, back in the bar, is a piece of shit.

14

The room is fine. It's how his life would be if he wasn't lifted up by outside agency: rudimentary, not quite safe. The door doesn't exactly lock but he doesn't exactly have any valuables. He sleeps on Fredo's sheets, washes himself in the filthy sink. Steel yourself is a funny phrase. Stiffen the sinews, eliminate vulnerability, evacuate feeling. Get up and go to work. He still hasn't fetched the Vespa, he'll have to catch the tram.

There are thunderheads on the horizon. A storm would be great. He can't remember what they are shooting. Is it still the travelling fair? He goes through the gates with his head down, greeting no one. Heads to the studio, sits at an easel. The painting he left two days ago is waiting for him. He squeezes out worms of paint. No one else is in yet. He picks up his brush, inhaling turpentine, and hears a voice behind him. Look what the cat dragged in. Hi, he says. Morning. Ettore said I should come in. Most people do, Dani says. That's sort of what a job is, coming in. Nicholas paints steadily, he doesn't look round. Good, he says. Here I am.

For the next couple of days, he stays in the workshop, taking on any task. Ageing forty tankards, sure, pass them over. He's sitting on the floor, Friday morning, drying them off, when Dani comes up behind him again. It would be really helpful, he says, if you could come on set. One of the translators has called in sick. He turns around. No one could be more impassive, more sarcastic than Danilo. Blue shirt. He knows it intimately, he ironed it himself. It would be my pleasure, he says, and follows Dani's furious back all the way to Studio 15.

It's even more chaotic than last week. Nicholas has missed the scene inside the belly of the whale, the giantess arm-wrestling for money as drunk men cheer her on, so many Jonahs in their cups. Today she is in her own quarters, as Casanova spies on her through a slit in the canvas. The tent is a masterpiece of strange detail. The giantess is like a sad animal, driven by her miniature attendants. She is supposed to play with her dolls, each one of them furnished with a tiny dress, and then get in a tub of water and sing a song while the attendants wash her. So much water in this film. But the boiler isn't working and Sandy refuses to take off her clothes. Sutherland is advocating for her, which is making the situation worse. Fellini has stopped speaking English at all and is just shouting at him in Italian. Does he know that Sutherland can understand? Nicholas looks at him under his lashes. Yes.

Dani walks right into the middle, takes Sutherland and bodily removes him. Read Voltaire, he says soothingly. I will fix her bath. Sandy is crying. She's so shy, she can't bear being at the centre of any situation. Nicholas catches one of her hands. Sandy, he says, let's leave them to it.

Come and eat a doughnut in the sun. They sit together outside, leaning their backs against the wall. She's the gentlest person he's ever met. I don't like doughnuts, she says. What I really want is an apple.

At last the water is warm. They go back in. Sandy sings her melancholy song. The attendants chatter, they slosh in with her. Fine, Fellini says. It's done. Sandy, you have a beautiful voice. Dani catches Nicholas's eye and winks, not warmly, but not coldly either. Then he walks out with an arm around Pinocchio's bony shoulders.

15

Nicholas is spending a lot of time in the boy bars. He could be drawing, he could be going to the museums but who the fuck cares is his motto now. He wants to be a little bit drunk all the time, and if there are other options, well, he's open to experiment too. He watches the boys peacocking up and down, pretending not to notice the men in the cars. None of them, they say loudly, would ever take it up the ass, but to accept a blow job from some poor fag for cash, you'd have to be a fool to turn down money that easy. Each time he hears a comment like this, his stomach fills with bile.

It's Sunday night when Pasolini appears. Maybe he came on foot, Nicholas can't see the Alfa. He's dressed just like the boys, the same wide collars, the same boots. Only his shirt is Missoni, it cost more than they make in a year. He hasn't seen Nicholas. The boys gather around him, just as they did in the villages outside Mantua. It's not that he's rich, it's that he likes them, he listens, he takes them seriously. Nicholas has seen him sitting with Rocco while the boy talked uninterruptedly for more than an hour about a motocross bike he wanted. What has Nicholas got to offer? Hello, I've been working on that translation of your poems, and by the way I'm homeless and a murderer, sort of.

He watches Pasolini chat with the boy in the red shirt, the dealer. They come to an agreement, they walk out. Nicholas orders a vodka, drinks it, orders another.

16

It's on a night like this that Ettore makes his proposition. He sits down, he lays his head against the table. I'm fucked, he says. Nicholas is so drunk he can hardly focus. You're where, he says. Ettore heaves himself up and comes back with an espresso, heavily sugared. Drink that, he says. I need to talk to you.

17

It's really simple, Ettore keeps saying. It's basically just what you did before. Except instead of dropping the reels off you pick them up. It isn't the same, Nicholas says. The sugar and the coffee have cleared his head, a bit. They're sitting at a table outside, not that it's any quieter. Horns and exhaust, the constant backdrop to nights in Rome.

It isn't the same because the reels were supposed to be dropped off and they aren't supposed to be picked up. Right? You're stealing them. I'm not stealing them, Ettore shouts. Nicholas has never seen him anything other than completely unflappable and this new distressed Ettore is disturbing. Look, it's not stealing. They just want to have them, and then they'll give them back. They're borrowing them. Oh great, so it's blackmail, Nicholas says. It's what, extortion? Ettore shrugs. I guess. It's a thing with Grimaldi, a Neapolitan thing, I don't know. Someone owes someone something, they don't get it, they do this, then it's all fine. It's a game. Everyone understands it.

What *I* don't understand, Nicholas says, is why you can't do it. Or Fredo. Fredo's gone away. Ettore looks like he's going to cry. Please Nico, we are so in the shit. Nothing will happen to you, I promise. The door will be open. You just go up there on the scooter, you walk in, you pick up a few reels, you walk out. That's it. What if they call the police, Nicholas asks. Oh please. Ettore shrugs, his entire body conveying his contempt for the police. You work at the studio. You're doing a pickup. What, Nicholas says, in the middle of the night? Ettore shrugs again. Movie people work strange hours. And you'll get paid. Please say yes.

It's obviously a stupid thing to do but then again there doesn't seem to be any reason not to do it. Who the fuck cares, remember. When, he asks. I don't know. They'll tell me. Sometime this week. Great, says Nicholas. Terrific. So now you've sobered me up perhaps you could buy me a drink.

18

It is the same, it's not the same. He takes the same road. It's later, quieter, there's no moon. He's riding Fredo's scooter, he's wearing Fredo's helmet. Also stupid, he thinks. He's probably the only person in Rome wearing one tonight. He has a feeling inside himself like when he first asked Alan for money. It's not reckless exactly, it's like he's checked out and someone colder, cooler has taken control. It's a job, he'll be paid, and then maybe he'll leave Rome altogether, find himself another new life.

There's something wrong with the scooter. It wobbles so hard it takes all his strength to keep it straight. He doesn't know enough to diagnose it. Anyway, he's here. He leaves it under a pine tree in the car park. It hadn't occurred to him that there might be dogs, a nightwatchman. He stands by the scooter, holding his breath, trying to listen. Cicadas, an occasional car. There's no one out there.

The front door is shut and he panics again, but when he presses the handle it opens smoothly. He's wearing his dirty plimsolls. The lights are off. He walks down the corridor in the dark. He hasn't thought this through at all. How will he find the reels without lights? He pushes the heavy door into the vault and to his relief the room is illuminated faintly by the refrigerator unit. It's so cold his breath is visible. He's been told to take reels from *Casanova* and *Salò*, and then something else, at random, so Grimaldi is not too obviously the target. He'll know, Ettore said, but everyone else will be confused.

Film is a preservative, he's heard that often enough. He's listened to Pasolini talk about it, how cinema harvests reality, gathering up what would otherwise decay and die. Film is captured time, time arrested. And now he can release it, unwind the clock, let it all go.

He has to remind himself that nothing is going to be destroyed. The reels will be safe, they will soon be back on the shelves. Still, he takes a moment to look at the labels, to consider what he's removing from the record. Dani's whale, his black plastic sea, based on the drawings they made together, sitting in a little boat on the Adriatic, when they had known each other less than a week. And from *Salò*, the big dance at the end, where for a moment he and Pasolini touched hands and then flinched away.

19

It's weird, he thought all hell would break loose at the studio, but nothing happens. A day goes by, another. Then he has the feeling that trouble has arrived. Work doesn't stop, but people are summoned to see Fellini, one by one. Not the staff, only the heads of department. When Dani leaves the office, he slams the door so hard a wall in the set downstairs falls down. He doesn't speak to anyone in the workshop, only Vito. Then Grimaldi comes in his big car. There is a second round of meetings. Vito enacts calmness, keeps the workshop ticking over. It's not until 27 August, a whole week after the reels went, that the story appears in the papers.

Also weird, Nicholas doesn't feel guilty or afraid. He joins the group crowding around the pages. I don't get it, someone says. Did it just happen or did they just find out? Is there a ransom, Gio asks. The only books he ever reads are *gialli*, cheap crime novels with their yellow covers. Calm down, Vito says, holding his hands out like a priest. Everyone get back to work. We don't pay ransoms here. If we did we'd never make a film again, it would happen every day. It's probably terrorists, Gio says hopefully. The Red Brigades, or the fascists. The next thing you know there'll be a bomb threat, and then a kidnap – He is silenced by Vito throwing a towel at his head. There won't be any kidnap. Rhino yes, kidnap no.

What Nicholas would like to do is speak to Danilo. He tells himself that it is because he requires information, but he knows that what he really wants is to speak to Danilo, just to pass words back and forth between their two mouths. He waits a day, he waits another day. It is common knowledge now that the scenes are missing and will have to be reshot. Dani is refusing, and anyway most of the actors have already gone home. They would have to be brought back from wherever they are: England, mostly, and in Sandy's case, Shelbyville, Indiana.

Everyone in the workshop has an opinion. You know, Vito says grievingly, that whale was the most beautiful thing that ever came out of this workshop. But if we reshoot, poor Donaldino will have to go in the river again. The flights must be more than the ransom, surely, Ettore says, but nobody seems to know what the ransom is.

Nobody seems to know where Danilo is, either. Nicholas goes out into the backlot, and finally sees him sitting alone by the Grand Canal. Hi, he says. He scuffs one plimsoll against the edge. I only wanted to see if you were okay. Those shoes are disgusting, Dani says. They should go in the bin. He lets his head fall back. Come on then, he says. Sit down if you must.

20

Neither of them apologizes. Neither of them even alludes to what has happened between them. They sit in silence, watching the water. Are you okay though, Nicholas says eventually. There is another long silence. Do you know what, Dani says. I'm actually relieved. I hated that shoot. I hated every minute of it. I don't even care about the whale. Did you hear what Fellini wants to do? He wants to insert a card saying *SCENES STOLEN*. Fine by me. I'm glad it's gone. He smiles at Nicholas, the first smile since the shoot started. Nicholas feels his own body responding, turning liquid. He has always found Dani in this mood irresistible. I'm going to say something crazy now, Dani says. Let's go away, right now. They can untangle this mess on their own. Let's go to Venice. Let's go and sit by the real Grand Canal. He looks at his watch. We could still make the last train. We could, Nicholas says. And so they do.

21

They stay in the same hotel as last year, but in a different room. It is even more beautiful, a cavern like a shell, tinted rose pink and della Robbia blue. The bed is enormous. But actually, Dani says, I'm going to fuck you against the window, with all the gondolas going by. Don't make a sound. If you do, everyone will see you. Nicholas can hear his own choked breaths. The prohibition, the exposure, above all the sense that Dani has returned: these things combine inside his body, creating an overwhelming torrent of arousal. I'm going to – he says, and ejaculates over green water.

Afterwards, they clean the glass together. Okay, Dani says, laughing as he bins the tissues. I'm willing to admit I did not think that one through.

22

In bed in Venice, Danilo dreams of Dresden. The loss of the reels has had the curious effect of bringing the film to life in a way that it wasn't before. It's resisting him, it is like a fish tugging on the line. For the first time it has entered his dreams, become a place to which he travels. It is no longer just Fellini's midlife crisis. It is his own autobiography too. It's a film about the cost of illusion. Casanova is not a rake in this version of the story, he is a person who is blinded by his own compelling story of himself. He is the Fool in a deck of tarot cards, condemned to draw the wrong conclusions, to misinterpret all the data. But if the film is an indictment of illusion, it is also an invitation to be seduced.

It must be after three. He climbs out of bed, looks for a moment at Nicholas's sleeping face, his damp red hair spread out across the pillow. That bloody boy, that beautiful boy. He is powerless against him. He knows it was wrong to bring another person into it the way he did, to use him as a human shield. Inelegant. Cruel. Perhaps he is both those things. What is sex really but the desire to ram yourself into someone else's interior, to make them a part of you. Love as Cupid with a honeycomb, painted by Cranach, love as a catastrophe. Nicholas's slender thighs, the dark red of his pubic hair: these things induce a desire so sharp it is physical pain. He thinks about waking him, knowing that right now whatever he asks for will be supplied. It is dangerous to want someone this much. He has always known it, from the very first night.

Nicholas whimpers in his sleep, and Danilo turns away from him. He sits at the desk by the window, listening to the water slapping outside. What he saw in his sleep, what he needs to draw, is the backdrop to the opera in Dresden. The version he has made isn't good enough, it is insufficiently beautiful. He understands what they are doing now. His job is to produce the seductions, and Fellini's job is to tear them down. The more formidable they are, the better the film.

23

They stay in Venice for three days. The city is soupy in the heat. Each morning they get the vaporetto to Lido, walk across the island to the beach. They pick out their favourite houses, watch families marshalling for the day, each child burdened with beach balls and towels. That one's queer, Dani says, nudging Nicholas. He will grow up to be a great costume designer. The child saunters, licking an ice cream, allowing a distance to grow between him and the quarrelsome crocodile of his siblings. Dani winks at him and to their amusement the little boy winks back.

Nicholas is reading a magazine article about Dirk Bogarde. He didn't get paid very much for *Death in Venice*, he reports. And his make-up at the end was cleaning fluid. I'll tell you something about that film, Dani says, stretching out on his lounger. Every single closet in the Polish family's rooms was filled with clothes. Not just any clothes. Historically perfect, beautiful clothes, right down to the underwear. And the drawers were never opened! Visconti thought the viewer would know they were there.

The water is green. They eat cherries. They swim. Everything is perfect, really.

24

On 1 September at eight in the morning they are back at Cinecittà. And we are not leaving again until we finish this film, Danilo says, clapping his hands together. His high spirits infect the workshop. What was down is up. Even the missing reels are no longer insurmountable. The lab has made a new negative from the positives. Not as good, Dani says, but better than pushing poor Donald in the Thames again. I don't know what a positive is, Nicholas says. I mean, I don't really know what a negative is. Tech stuff, Dani says. Why would you? The negative is the original recording. The positive is the copy. But if you need to strike more prints you can damage the negative, so you reverse the process. You can do it indefinitely. Nicholas has an image of film replicating, duplicating itself, a proliferation of images without end. So it's all okay, he asks. *Salò* too? *Salò* no, Dani says. *Salò* is a fuck-up. They hadn't made a work print from some of those endings. Normally Pasolini shoots so much, there would be infinite material. You know how much he shot for *Oedipus Rex*? 70,000 metres. That's 67,000 metres of overshoot! But with this one, he practically edited in the camera. There was no overshoot. I don't know what he's going to do. Not reshoot. Make do, I guess. Use a different version for the ending. He's devastated, Sergio said. He loved the one where we all danced.

They walk together to Studio 15. The travelling fair is gone, packed up and put away. In its place is Dresden Opera House. It's very simple: a single flat with layer upon layer of balustrades and boxes, each with its own door. Nicholas's task is to put three thousand candles into chandeliers. Come on, lazy donkeys, Dani says, pulling Ettore along by his shirt. I'll show you how I want the first one and you two can do the rest.

It's chilly in the studio. The breeze-block walls lock out the heat. Danilo has returned to the workshop, to oversee the corrections to his backdrop. There is no one else in earshot. What the fuck is happening, Nicholas hisses. Is this what was meant to happen? I don't know, Ettore says. It's not our problem. You did your job, we're not involved now. He doesn't look convinced. It really is better if you just forget it. And to illustrate, he spends the rest of the morning diligently setting candles into another and then another chandelier.

Okay, says Danilo, coming to check their work after lunch. So now you light them all and let them burn until the drips underneath are as long as the candles. No more, no less. You are not going to believe how beautiful this scene will be. Everything I learned at La Scala, it's all going in. Visconti has nothing on me!

They go home late, they come back to the studio at dawn the next morning. It's cold at first light. The extras are walking around in powdered wigs and gowns, with their own coats clutched incongruously over the top. It's like encountering the end of a party, seeing people pour out of the canteen in their night-time finery, with cups of coffee in their hands. Nicholas watches as a woman in a cape made of hundreds of rosettes of cream-coloured lace bends forward to light a cigarette. Don't set fire to my robe, *signora*, Danilo says as he passes. You will break both the budget and my heart.

It takes the entire workshop to move the backdrop to the studio. Danilo oversees the hanging while Nicholas runs back to the canteen to get a tray of cakes. Everyone needs cosseting today. They have arranged themselves around Dani like a protective shoal. Whatever he requires is done without the need for speech. Nicholas has never seen the workshop function at such a high gear.

He gets back moments before Fellini is due. The backdrop is up. At the centre is a giant gold sun with beaten metal rays, set against a sky the colour of a peach. In front are the ramparts of a city, topped with statues and tinted the mauve of evening. It is camp and gorgeous, completely absurd. When the lights go up, the whole thing glows. Watch this, Dani says. He tugs a mechanism and the disc of the sun creaks opens, creating a golden platform for a golden figure to appear. Fellini comes up behind Danilo and kisses him on the top of his head. Maestro, he says. They say it to me, but the name belongs to you.

25

The opera takes a long time to film. It is done in two parts, to be spliced together later. There is the performance itself, the chorus with their swords and helmets, their breastplates and cumbersome wings. Then there is the audience. Some are in boxes, but most, Casanova included, are standing in the main hall. The floor has to be raked, so that everyone is visible for the camera, but this makes it almost impossible to walk on in the cumbersome heels of eighteenth-century shoes. One extra stumbles and twists her ankle, mid-shot. For fuck's sake, Dani mutters. It's easier working with horses.

At the end, the golden sun opens, the golden figure prances on his platform. The audience applaud, then turn in silence for the royal family to file out. Everyone leaves. Only Casanova remains, smiling to himself in his brown silk cloak, hopeful of an assignation. There is a creaking sound. He looks up as the lit chandeliers descend around him. Men come out in brown jerkins and caps, carrying enormous black beaters. They set the chandeliers spinning, they flap the beaters until all the candles are snuffed out. The chandeliers are winched back up. Then the men file out, quick march, quick march, leaving Casanova alone in the half-dark.

That scene, Dani says, leaning against the scaffolding, is the one that people will remember.

26

Sutherland has rented Roman Polanski's old villa, but really he's living in make-up or on set. There isn't a single scene that doesn't include him, and there isn't a single scene in which Fellini is nice to him. Nicholas sees him one day out on the lot, tap-dancing with a child he doesn't recognize. It must be one of the extras. He looked lonely and sort of deranged, Nicholas tells Dani that evening. I think it might be good if you talk to him sometimes, Dani says. It's hard not being able to communicate. You get lost in your own head.

After this, Nico takes to dropping by make-up in the morning, bringing a coffee or a paper. After a week, he is invited to visit the dressing room. He sits on the daybed while Sutherland is fastened into a sugar-pink suit. The man is obsessed with cinema. He's a fan, a bona fide buff. When he finds out that Nicholas worked on *Salò* he bombards him with questions. Is Pasolini a communist? Is he a pederast? Is he a genius? What do you think of his films?

Yes, no, yes, says Nicholas. I think so, anyway. They go through the films together, acting out favourite scenes. Sutherland loves the bit in *The Decameron* when Ninetto falls into a latrine. *Aiuto, aiuto, sono caduto nella merda*, he cries. What lightness! No American director could have made that scene! He is pompous but also adorable, like a big dog embarrassed by its size. Why don't we go and see one tonight, he says, thumping Nicholas's shoulder in his enthusiasm. There's got to be a Pasolini film on in Mamma Roma!

The only one they can find in the paper is *Oedipus Rex*. Sutherland's driver drops them off. Nicholas thinks how strange it is that this is the first time he's been to the cinema since he came to Italy. Danilo never goes. Don't tell anyone, he says, but I prefer the opera. Cinema hurts my eyes.

He's seen the film before, at least once, maybe twice. It is different now that he knows Pasolini. He doesn't try to follow the story. He watches the images and he feels the emotions, allowing the two streams to interact inside him.

Silvana Mangano is so beautiful, Sutherland whispers. Watch how she never moves her face. The opening section of the film is set in Friuli during the war. Jocasta and Laius are based on Pasolini's parents. Someone, it must have been Dani, told Nicholas that Mangano wore Susanna's own dresses from the period. The little boy is Pier Paolo himself, dark-eyed, irresistible.

Then the film switches to an ancient world. The little boy is hung from a stick and carried into the desert. He is abandoned, he is rescued. Now he is a man, with a hurt face and uncomprehending eyes. He sees the oracle, he is given the prophecy. From now on he is a tainted person, a person who has no home and who cannot find love. Nicholas understands only too well what this film is really about.

The drama rolls through its inevitable cycles. There could be no other ending. Oedipus kills the stranger at the crossroads, marries the bereaved queen. He is told what he has done and he refuses to believe it. At last he accepts that he has killed his own father, that he is the murderer for whom he hunts, the person who must be driven into exile. Oedipus' rages are terrifying. He can't act, Sutherland whispers, and yet he could not be bettered in this role.

Jocasta hangs herself, Oedipus thrusts the knife into his eyes. Then the frame switches again. They are in a city, perhaps Bologna, blind Oedipus and his angelic guide, played by big shambling irrepressible Ninetto. It is the present day. It kind of petered out there, Sutherland says afterwards, when they are drinking in the bar. With him just wandering off into a field. Oh, says Nicholas, surprised. Didn't it just wind back to the beginning? Wasn't that where it started? He sees the film like a loop, a series of descending circles, crime and redemption eating their own tail. Boy would I like to work with him, Sutherland says wistfully. And he'll never use me. I think too much and I'm too technical. I'm useless in Italy.

27

It's very odd, Dani says. I hated this film for over a year, and now I love it. Every element gives me pleasure. I think we have finished the Piombi. Do you want to come and see? Do you remember? It's what you drew for me the first day we met.

And I fainted, Nicholas says. And you revived me with cordial and then you took me back to your bed and made me do such disgraceful things. Nicholas! Dani cries. You made me! I was being a good nurse that day! They look at each other. Danilo blinks like a happy cat. Come on, I want to show you, he says, and takes Nicholas by the hand.

The Piombi is appalling, even in this pantomime version. The cell is so small you can't stand up inside it. The door has the same locks and bolts that Nicholas drew that first morning. Look, Dani says. I put in the graffiti you copied on the wall. He has also made the roof, the great lead roof that gives the prison its name. It's over this that Casanova will crawl when he makes his great escape.

It's terrifying, Nico says. It's brilliant, but it makes me feel ill.

For the filming of the prison scenes, Sutherland has grown a beard. He sits huddled in his cell, nearly naked, his head touching his knees. He's a tall man. The takes get longer. It is evident that he's in pain but he refuses to complain, to ask for special treatment. He takes being an actor so seriously.

28

Dani always has to be one step ahead of production. While Sutherland is imprisoned in the Piombi, he is busy refining his next creation: the automaton Rosalba, the mechanical doll with whom Casanova will fall in love. Rosalba is played by a real ballerina. They have tried all kinds of make-up, but nothing has the right porcelain quality. In the end they take a cast, covering her face in plaster-soaked bandages. They make a mask from it, so that she wears her own frozen features, unnaturally shining. She comes for a fitting in October, and shows them the moves she's been inventing. It's eerie, watching her, as she jolts and lurches stiffly round the room.

29

An ugly thing happens that month. Nicholas hears about it in the workshop, carries the news to Danilo. Pasolini was driving through the centre of town, in the Piazza di Spagna, when some boys dragged him from his car and beat him with chains. What, says Dani. What did you say?

They both go over to the house that evening. It is the first time they have visited together. There are other people there. Nico recognizes the blonde woman from the New Year dinner, greets Ninetto with a hug. Pasolini is on the red sofa, dark glasses on indoors. His face is bruised. It's nothing, he keeps saying. A misunderstanding. I am fine. His mother stoops over him, little like a bird. Pasolini reaches up, kisses her powdered cheek. So this is Susanna.

On the way home, Dani is preoccupied. He waits until they are inside the flat, pours them both drinks. I don't think that was about sex, he says. I think it's a warning. A warning from who, Nicholas asks. Why would anyone want to hurt Pasolini, he's so gentle. Dani frowns. I don't think you pay attention to anything at all, he says. Have you read a newspaper since you've been here? Did you understand nothing about *Salò*?

I thought *Salò* was about the war, Nicholas says. You both told me that. You laughed at me because I didn't know what it was.

Oh boy. Dani strikes his own leg, just lightly. Not really. No. It's about now. It's all about now. He goes to his study, digs around in his desk and comes back with a newspaper article, cut out with scissors. There are lots, he says, but this one I kept.

It's by Pasolini. The date is last November. You didn't tell me about this, Nico says. I was living here then. I hardly knew you, Dani says. And you didn't know anything about Italy. You hadn't even met Pasolini.

The article is titled 'What is this coup d'état? I know'. The same phrase is repeated throughout. *Io so*, I know. It seems to Nicholas that he is reading an indictment of an entire political class, perhaps even a whole society. Pasolini claims in his calm, reasonable, apocalyptic way that he knows who is responsible for great crimes, for the massacres in Milan in 1969, and in Brescia and Bologna in 1974. He knows who is responsible for the attempted coup. He talks about fascists and anti-communist crusades in Italy, about the secret role of the Church and the CIA. He talks about important people using hired killers, street thugs, to do their work and he goes on to say that everybody else knows these things, too, but they all refuse to speak, so as to preserve a world that is already unliveable. He asserts the purity of the Italian Communist Party. He says: The intellectual courage to speak the truth and the practice of politics are two irreconcilable things in Italy.

It is a petrol bomb in paper form. Fucking hell, Nicholas says when he gets to the end. Is it true? I don't know as much as Pasolini, Dani says, but yes, I think it's true. He doesn't just see the evil deeds. That would be easy. What he sees is how we all turn a blind eye to evil because we are comfortable and we want to stay that way. We are sleepwalkers like the children in *Salò* are sleepwalkers. He attacks modernity, he puts it on trial. He thinks consumerism is a new fascism because there is so much violence hidden inside it, because it destroys nature and natural behaviour. It's the same as *Salò*. The articles are a denunciation of power. They are making him famous, but I think they are also putting him in danger. I don't know, Nico. It's like a disease, he is compelled to speak the truth. And I am a coward and I am afraid of what the cost will be.

30

But these are other people's problems, frankly. Nicholas shrugs them off, they remain peripheral. The fact is that this is the happiest autumn of his life. He walks all the time. The trees turn yellow. The light is wild, it touches everything. He loves his work. And then at night, there is Dani, a foreign sea. He didn't know – but there seems all of a sudden no limits to the things he didn't know. In the past this was a source of terror. Now, it's joy.

31

The rain comes, followed by a run of cool, bright days. I'm going to go to my mother's for All Saints' Day, Dani says. Just for lunch. Or no, maybe I'll stay the night. Will you come? Nico, come, she'd love it. Not to sound like you, Nicholas says, but I actually think I have to work this weekend. Isn't it Casanova's threesome at the inn on Sunday? Ettore and I still haven't finished ageing the bed.

They eat breakfast together, bread and eggs. I'd like to go to Mantua, Nicholas says. Maybe we could both go at Christmas. Did you put a bay leaf in this omelette, Dani says, pulling something out of his mouth. It's not generally done. And yes, I would like that. Lots of cake and single beds, very festive. Before he leaves he pulls Nicholas into his arms. I'm glad you're here, he says. I am happy you are back. It's the only acknowledgment he has ever made of the breach between them.

Nicholas rides to work. His hands are cold, he needs gloves. The yellow leaves reflected in green water, it's too much. Too sweet, too delicious. He holds his fortune in his heart, he gives up his body to the traffic. Most people today are seeing their families. He finds Fellini and the director of photography blocking out the tavern scene. Sutherland is in his dressing room, lying on the daybed, reading Proust. I have my Casanova face on, he says, so don't make me laugh.

Ettore isn't in yet. Nicholas has the workshop to himself. He makes coffee, he sits in the doorway to drink it. He finds his mask, puts it on, gets the brushes and sets about the bed, just as Dani showed him. It's more like a room than a bed, enclosed with wooden shutters. Ettore appears at ten. Don't shout at me, he says. It's a big family day. I can't just disappear. My mum says I can stay for an hour, but then I have to go home. Your mum isn't actually the boss of the workshop, Nicholas says and Ettore rolls his eyes. Sure, he says. But she's the boss of me.

They each have a hammer, they each have nails, in several different sizes. They work their way round on their hands and knees, creating the illusion of woodworm. Okay, Ettore says. I have to go or she'll roast me instead of the meat. He stops in the doorway, hesitates, comes back. I don't know if I should say this, he says. But they're giving the reels back to your friend tonight. There's a handover.

I don't understand, Nicholas says. I thought they needed a ransom. Was it paid? Ettore shrugs. I don't think so. I don't know. The message was – The message, Nicholas says. What message? What the fuck is going on, Ettore? Ettore's face has shut tight. The message was that you should probably go, just check that it all goes okay. One of the Termini kids is taking him. Just go to the bar, keep an eye, that's all.

I don't want to, Nicholas says. I'm busy, and Ettore shrugs again. If it was me, he says, I guess I'd go.

Alone in the workshop, Nicholas washes his brushes. His hands are shaking. Every time he gets ahead he's pulled back by the stupid things an earlier Nicholas, that defective model, seems to have done. He doesn't want to go. He hasn't been back to the bars for weeks. But then if the reels are given back, it's like the slate is wiped clean. All afternoon he weighs it up, going forward and back. Ettore didn't even give him a time. No one will be out before ten. Maybe he should see a film first.

Instead he goes home and runs himself a bath. He lights a candle, and lies there with the shadows jumping. All Saints, All Souls, the moment in the year when the veil between the world of the living and the dead is at its thinnest. He thinks for the first time in months of Alan, and for the first time ever it occurs to him that he might not have been the only reason for his death. A double life is hard to bear. Maybe, he, Nicholas, is not exclusively to blame.

The water is cooling. He heaves himself up, leaves a tidal wave of water on the floor, a wet towel on the bed. You live like a pig, Nico, says Dani's voice in his head. He puts on a sweater, borrows Dani's gloves and coat. If he has to go he has to go.

The bar is heaving. He moves in and out of groups he half knows. He doesn't even want a drink. He gets an espresso and takes it outside, says hello to the queens by the door. It isn't long before the Alfa appears. Pasolini doesn't get out. He opens the window, winding it halfway. Two of the girls sashay over, patting their wigs. Oh come on, a boy shouts. He doesn't want what you've got. The taller queen turns round, looks him up and down. And you do, honey, she says, but to be honest it would scare you into next week.

Pasolini dismisses them, but politely, courteously. He beckons to the group behind, five or six boys. They're vaguely familiar, all dressed in the uniform, fiddling with their hair. He singles one out, they chat. Then something is agreed, because the boy is going round into the street, opening the door on the other side.

Nicholas hops off his stool, slides through the crowd to his scooter. It's just like before. The anxiety is gone. Someone more competent, more cool is in control.

All the same, it's not easy following a car through Saturday night Rome, even on a Vespa. He trails them down Via Cavour and round the Colosseum. The memory of the gold-toothed boy and his brother surges up. There are other things he could be doing tonight. They go straight past the Palatine and Circo Massimo. Are they heading to Testaccio? No, the silver car keeps going, down through Ostiense and on to the SP8. He understands now. They're heading for Ostia and the sea.

He's never followed a car before. It's like dancing, keeping his distance, slowing when they do, guessing ahead. He's so sure he knows where they're going that he almost misses the indicator signalling a right. They stop at a roadside restaurant, and Nicholas parks under a tree. He must be there for half an hour, breathing fumes. He can see them inside, two dark figures silhouetted against a rectangle of light. What he is doing is gross, beyond undignified.

At last they get up. They go back out to the car. He kicks the scooter to make it start. It's the same road he took to the football, the road that turns into a track and goes past shacks, running parallel to the river. He follows them cautiously, keeping well back. He's sure they're going to the same field. Even so, he almost overshoots. The car is parked on the dirt. Again the two figures are illuminated. He watches them talking, sees Pasolini smile.

There must have been a negotiation. Then Pasolini lowers his head in the direction of the boy's crotch. Nicholas almost hears it inside himself, a hiss like when a record comes to an end. What is he doing here? He doesn't need to stay and watch. Fuck the reels. Let the man get laid in peace. He has his own life. He paddles the scooter over the grass with his feet, turns around on the track and rides back in the direction of the city.

ACT 4

I RESTI

1

He gets up in the dark, pulls his socks on, borrows Dani's sheepskin again and heads out to the studio. The sun is rising. His whole body is suffused with happiness. He has been granted an absolution, he has been given the gift of understanding what he has. Not everyone gets that. Dani querulous, Dani laughing, Dani in his obscenely tight swimming trunks. He isn't due back from Mantua until late morning. Nico runs to the cafeteria, buys him a *maritozzo*, one of those split buns stuffed with cream, leaves it on his desk. Should he write something? No. The bun is enough.

2

Today they are working on the threesome scene. It takes place in the giant bed. When Nicholas arrives, the shutters are closed. Fellini has persuaded one of the actresses to go in there with the chief electrician and feign the act of love. Why does he do these things?

Sutherland comes in from make-up. The actress is supposed to pick him up and fling him on the bed but now she has gone behind the door of the inn and is sitting in the dark. Fellini goes in after her. Presumably they are talking. Then he comes out, opening the door so that everyone can see, and says at the top of his voice, this woman hasn't been fucked for four years. Her face flames. She gets up. Now do the scene, Fellini says. He grabs her breasts with both hands. In retaliation, she squeezes his crotch, his little fig. He smiles at her. Now. Now you can do the scene. The worst thing about it is he's right.

In the middle of the take, Fellini's secretary runs over. She whispers in his ear. Then other people are coming in, then all going out together. What's happening? The camera is still running. Nicholas walks towards the door. The men are standing in their coats. It's Pasolini, someone says. Then Danilo comes up. He goes straight to Fellini, clutches him like a child. It takes Nicholas a moment to realize that both men are sobbing.

3

The radio is saying that there has already been an arrest, that a kid called Pelosi was picked up driving erratically in a silver Alfa. The radio says that Pasolini has been beaten to death, that his body was found on a waste ground in Ostia.

A trick gone wrong, is the instant verdict.

Please, Nicholas thinks. Please let it be that. He has the sense that he is made entirely of ash, like the ash of a cigarette that still holds its shape even though it is nothing, the negative of a positive, pure remains.

4

The phone has rung all night. Nicholas makes cups of tea that aren't drunk, goes out in the dark at six to get the papers. They all have the same picture on the front. It's like something Sergio might have made. It isn't a person. It's a brutality. It's what bodies are when they aren't. They tore his fucking ear off, Dani says. There are tyre marks on his vest. His hair is solid with blood. Don't look at these, Nicholas says. It's disgusting. It's my friend, Dani says, and takes the paper back.

5

The boy confesses. He says that Pasolini wanted him to do something he didn't want to do, that he tried to penetrate him with a wooden stick. Oh please, Danilo says. Who can believe this shit. I'll tell you who. The whole fucking world.

The boy says Pasolini attacked him, that his expression was so wild it was terrifying. He says that he only tried to defend himself. I lost my head, he says. *Ho perduto la testa.* He is seventeen. *Il Messaggero* prints a photograph of him, posing in a sweater, his shadow hunched behind him. The headline describes him as a *ragazzo di vita*. The phrase is the title of Pasolini's famous first novel. The implication is clear. These are the boys Pasolini championed and chased, and here are the consequences: death on a construction site, while normal people were asleep in their beds.

By Tuesday, the papers are reporting that he didn't die from the blows, that he was killed later, run over by his own car. His heart burst.

Do you know how many trials Pasolini went through, Danilo asks. Nicholas doesn't. Thirty-three. Rape, corruption, whatever they could think of. One man said Pasolini robbed him with a gun loaded with golden bullets. This is exactly the same. I don't know what happened but it wasn't this.

6

Today the radio is full of the news of Pasolini's last interview. It is reported that he chose the title himself, asking that it be called 'We are all in danger'. It is being described as prophetic. Do you want to read it, Nicholas asks. I can go and get it. Yes, says Dani. No. Yes.

It is in *La Stampa*. Nicholas buys the paper, brings it home. He doesn't go to Fagiani, he doesn't buy cakes. They read it together, sitting at the kitchen table. The introduction explains that the interview took place on All Saints' Day, between four and six in the evening, a few hours before Pasolini was killed.

What he says is a warning. It is a warning about the world, about what he calls the power machine and how it is affecting every aspect of society. Pasolini says that violence happens on all levels of society. He says the poor might use a metal bar and the rich a stock-exchange manoeuvre.

He says that he descends into hell. He says that he brings back the truth.

What is the truth, the journalist asks. That we want to own everything at any price, Pasolini says.

He says: I think that, in one way or the other, we are all weak because we are all victims. And we are all guilty, because we are all ready to play at slaughtering each other, as long as we are able to own everything at the end of the slaughter.

He describes the alternative. The world will become a larger place.

He says: Everything becomes ours and we won't need the stock exchange, the board of directors or the metal bar to steal from each other.

He says that he is not interested in the culpability of individuals. He says that it is a total system.

He says: What I mean is, I go down to hell and I discover things that do not bother other people. But be careful. Hell is rising and it's coming at you.

He says: Everybody knows that, as a person, I do pay for what I say. But there are also my books and my films that end up paying for me. Maybe I'm wrong after all, but I keep on thinking that we are all in danger.

The journalist asks him how he thinks he, Pasolini, can avoid this danger, this risk. It is getting dark, there is no light on in the room where they are talking. Pasolini says he will think about the question overnight, that he will answer in the morning. But in the morning he is dead.

7

Even this, Dani says. Even this will be used against him. He has been assassinated in the cleverest way imaginable. If they had shot him, he would be a martyr. But this: it looks as if he went out hunting for his own death. He describes the disgusting reality of the world and what they will say is that he wanted it to be so. That he was a low life who deserved what came for him. That what he wanted was the metal bar. They have killed *Salò* too. Perhaps that was the intention. Now people will watch it and they will say it was his dirty fantasy, and what he was trying to tell them will be lost. They will say he was a masochist who loved death. They will say he was a sadist who deserved what he got and they will make that kid a hero. Who killed Pasolini? I will tell you. Everyone.

Me, thinks Nicholas. Inadvertent or not, he was the accessory, it was he who supplied the lure. He understands why he was invited to Ostia now. The same reason the boy has confessed to something he almost certainly hasn't done. Because violence buys silence. Because most people, not Pasolini, are ruled by fear.

8

The funeral is on Wednesday. It is at the Campo de' Fiori, where the market is held. The entire square is packed with people. Nicholas will never forget the sight of the coffin being carried through the crowd. The boys have come, the boys in their jeans. The boys Pasolini fucked, the boys he listened to, found jobs for, helped, the boys he insisted on putting at the centre of the story. Some of them are impassive, but others, men too, raise their fists as the coffin passes.

9

Afterwards, they go back to the flat. I'd like to burn this suit, Danilo says. I will never wear it again. He sits at the kitchen table. I want to say such stupid things. He was my friend. This is the worst day of my life and tomorrow will be too. Pasolini would be ashamed of how banal I am. Nobody could ever be ashamed of you, Dani, Nicholas says. He knows that these are their last moments together, that the clock has run down. Pasolini understood everything about what was coming, and he was totally blind. The only thing he can do now is leave. He has been like Oedipus in the film, incapable of recognizing the harm he has done. Does it matter that he never intended any of it? No. Nicholas would tear his own eyes out too, if it would help anyone, but if he did he would be without the sight of Dani, who even now is walking towards him, even now is reaching out his arms. Love is the punishment, the final twist.

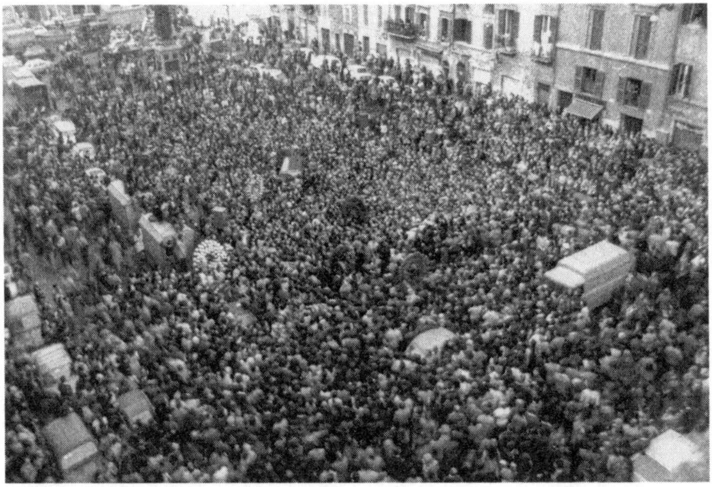

10

London is as hot as Rome. Hotter, maybe. Nicholas is sweating into his shirt. He ducks into the Curzon, just to be off the street. *Casanova* is playing. He has never seen it. He sits in the dark and he watches his own life unfold. There's Sandy singing in the tub, there's the boat that broke in two. There are whole sections he never saw made, but even they are filled with things he knows. Casanova's pink coat. Danilo's magic mirror, the ridiculous rhino that Ettore was so proud of. Perhaps his paintings are at the back of a set, he can't tell. He understands now why Fellini tortured Sutherland. The pleading quality, the uncertainty, it all bled into the role. What he is watching is someone who has no idea of who they are, who is living inside the wrappers of a dream. In the final sequence, Casanova waltzes on a frozen Grand Canal with the automaton Rosalba, the only woman he ever loved. The grey ice is pure Danilo: illusion for its own sake, longing and regret held in perfect suspension. The Rialto Bridge is draped in false snow. A cinema of paper and scissors, Fellini once called it. Every choice he has made was wrong except one. But Dani is a definite person and Nicholas is an indefinite person. He will probably live for ever. The house lights have come on, exposing worn red velvet. Nicholas gets up. He has brought nothing with him. He leaves the cinema, goes out into the sun.

Image Credit

Pasolini's funeral in Piazza Campo de' Fiori in Rome, 1975 © De Bellis Historical Archive/Fotogramma.

Quotations

150 'The principle . . . bloodshed. Baudelaire': *Salò*, dir. Pier Paolo Pasolini (1975).

157 'I want to show . . . "the other"': *Salò: Yesterday and Today*, dir. Amaury Voslion (2002).

158 'what my ambiguous love of liberty was against': Pier Paolo Pasolini, *In Danger: A Pasolini Anthology*, ed. and trans. Jack Hirschman (City Lights Books, 2010), p. 220.

178 'The greatest tragedy . . . of your desires': *Fellini's Casanova*, dir. Federico Fellini (1976).

179 'Sex is a pretext'

'Anoints with seed and then departs'

'A boy . . . the world's fecundity': Pier Paolo Pasolini, *Selected Poems*, trans. Norman MacAfee with Luciano Martinengo (John Calder, 1984), p. 211.

218 'The intellectual courage . . . irreconcilable things in Italy': Pier Paolo Pasolini, 'Cos'è questo golpe? Io so', *Corriere della Sera*, 14 November 1974, author's translation.

232–3 'I think . . . end of the slaughter'

'Everything becomes ours . . . to steal from each other'

'What I mean is . . . coming at you'

'Everybody knows . . . we are all in danger': Pier Paolo Pasolini, 'Siamo tutti in pericolo', *La Stampa*, 8 November 1975, in *Pasolini: The Massacre Game, Terminal Film, Text, Words, 1974–75*, ed. Stephen Barber, trans. Anna Battista (Clash City Sermons, 2021), pp. 49–53.

Author's Note

This is a work of fiction. Many of the characters in this book have their origins in real people, and some of the events described did happen, though no doubt not quite like this. The exact circumstances of Pasolini's death, and the role the missing reels played in it, remain mysterious. My own feeling is that while it's important to identify the individuals or group responsible, it risks missing the point of Pasolini's warnings about a system in which we are all enmeshed, and which has only grown more powerful in the past half-century.

Thank You

I wrote most of this book at the British School at Rome. Thanks to all, especially Christine Martin, Antonio Palmieri and Abigail Brundin.

A huge thank-you to Clara Tosi Pamphili, Roberto Valeriani, Jacopo Gilone and especially the maestro Luigi Piccolo for talking to me about Donati and sharing the extraordinary costumes at Sartoria Farani, a place I loved so much I borrowed its current location and inhabitants, moving them back half a century.

For help with research and contacts: John Craig, whose family history illuminated some of the illusions on which cinema once depended, Lauren Kassell and David Dernie for Pasqua etc., M. Cristiana Costanzo, Kevin Macdonald, Eugenia Paulicelli, JD Rhodes, Jerry Stafford and Tilda Swinton <3

A cordial at Florian to Chantal Joffe, for taking me to Venice and being my first reader.

The early readers: Ian Patterson, Francesca Segal, Matt Wolf, Richard Porter, Lauren J. Joseph, Denise Laing, Kitty Laing, Charlie Porter, Joseph Keckler and Luke Syson. And a special thank-you to Chiara Barzini, who unlocked Rome and cinema in so many ways, not least by taking my photo on the Isola Tiberina before this book was even thought of.

Rebecca Carter, *la migliore: grazie per tutto*. A dream to work together on this one. PJ Mark, for everything. Tilda Butterworth, crisis typesetter of dreams. At PEW: Margaret Halton and Alex Chernova, thank you for everything you do. And of course Sam Talbot and Kitty Malton, with much love and gratitude.

At Hamish Hamilton: Simon Prosser, my editor after all these years, Hermione Thompson, who stepped into the breach, Anna Ridley, Roz Hutchison, Chloe Davies, Rose Poole, Natalie Chapman, Caroline Pretty, Emma Brown, Ruby Fatimilehin, Preena Gadher and all at Penguin. A special thank-you to Richard Bravery for his sublime cover design.

At Il Saggiatore: the exceptional Luca Formenton, Sara Panzera, Rebecca Pignatiello, Giulia Feroleto and Alice Farina. A special thank you to Katia Bagnoli, the most thoughtful translator and fact checker extraordinaire.

At FSG: Marvellous Mitzi Angel, Emma Chuck, Na Kim for her gorgeous design, Sarita Varma, Lauren Hutton, Daniel del Valle, Pauline Post and all the team for their energy and hard work.

And thank you to everyone whose job it is to make and sell books. We're all of us indebted to you.